I0591324

THE PERFECT PERFUME AND OTHER TALES

9 FANTASTICAL VICTORIAN STORIES

ANTHEA SHARP

Fiddlehead Press

The Perfect Perfume and Other Tales ©February 2019 by Fiddlehead Press.

The Airship Adventures of Captain Jane Fury ©2018. Originally published in *Fiction River: Pulse Pounders, Adrenaline* in November 2018.

The Sun Never Sets ©2015. Originally published in *Alt.History 101*, July 2015

The Visit ©2017. Originally published in *Fiction River: Feel the Fear* in September 2017.

Pocket Full of Ashes ©2017. Originally published in *Fiction River: Superpowers* in November 2017.

Lady Elizabeth's Betrothal Ball ©2016. Originally published in *Fiction River: Last Stand* in November 2016.

The Worth of Rubies ©2013.

The Clockwork Harp ©2016. Originally published in *Fiction River: Haunted* in September 2016

The Perfect Perfume ©2015. Originally published in *Fiction River: Alchemy and Steam* in May 2015.

All rights reserved. No part of this book may be reproduced in any form or by any electronic or mechanical means, including information storage and retrieval systems, without written permission from the author, except for the use of brief quotations in a book review.

Cover by Ravven
Interior Artwork by Tairlei
Professional editing by Editing720.
Visit www.antheasharp.com

QUALITY CONTROL:
We care about producing error-free books. If you discover a typo or formatting issue, please contact antheasharp@hotmail so that it may be corrected.

THE AIRSHIP ADVENTURES
OF CAPTAIN JANE FURY

The deck of the airship tilts sharply, sending us careening through the clouds. I lunge for the wheel and spin it hard as the rear engine coughs out gouts of sickly steam. With a stomach-squeezing lurch, the HMS Minotaur loses more altitude.

Bracing my feet against the steering blocks, I wrestle the ship back to level.

"Get that propeller stabilized," I yell into the engine-room speaking tube.

"Aye, captain," my engineer calls back, her voice echoing through the long tube. "Nearly got her done."

I check to make sure my crew is strapped in. They're secure enough—I've some of the best airmen in the skies sailing with me. I glance at my new cabin boy. He roped in at the first sign of trouble, and now clings to the netting covering the cases of brandy we're transporting.

"All right?" I call.

He gives me a quick nod. The lad seems to be holding on well enough to his lunch—and his dignity—along with the net. Dirigible destabilization is a hard way to get your air legs, but a storm's worse.

"Keep your eyes peeled for sky monsters, boy," one of my crew tells him, half-joking.

Most lubbers think the air serpents are mere imaginings, and the Sky Kraken just a myth. But up here in the clouds, we know better.

"They don't really exist," the lad says, voice brave.

I don't try and convince him otherwise. Better if he never finds out the truth.

"The monsters we need to worry about now are blood-thirsty raiders," I say, keeping the wheel steady under my hands.

The rear engine catches again, then settles into a steady hum. I let out an imperceptible breath of relief as the Minotaur evens out.

Too bad the malfunction dropped us right in the path of the biggest thunderstorm I've ever seen.

The mass of cumulus clouds roil before us, a dark wall stitched with flashes of lightning. I stare at the storm, weighing our options.

My navigator hurries up, a rolled chart in his hand. "Alter our course, captain?"

He hands the chart to my first mate, William, who has just returned from helping in the engine room.

I glance to starboard. The shore of Portugal, which we paralleled for a time, has disappeared. Only the innocuous blue of the ocean winks and glitters at me. If we fall out of the sky, it'll be death by drowning. Is that better than crashing into the hard earth?

I generally try not to contemplate such things, but with

such precious cargo aboard it's hard not to be conscious of the danger.

"William, how far does that bank stretch, by your reckoning?" I tip my chin at the clouds.

My first mate studies the storm, his expression hard. "A good twenty kilometers."

"We must make London in time for the coronation. Even in clear weather, we don't have much leeway."

"Going through the storm would cause heavy damage," he says.

Unfortunately, he's right.

"Take the wheel," I say.

Once he does, I hold my gloved hand out to the navigator. "Chart."

Paper in hand, I stride to the netted cargo and spread the chart out. The navigator joins me and the cabin boy cranes his neck, curious.

"Here." I sketch a line with my thumb. "Chart a course back toward Spain. We can't risk being blown out over the open ocean."

My navigator sucks his teeth. "Is it wise, captain? There be..." He leans closer, throwing a look at the cabin boy, and says in a low voice, "Pirates."

I know there are pirates. But the alternatives are worse. Clenching my jaw, I give my navigator a hard stare. "Just do it."

"Aye, sir." He snatches his chart and hurries away to make the calculations.

The wind's rising, whipping a strand of dark hair across my face. I shove it back under my leather helmet and scowl at the clouds blocking our perfect route to England. Under other circumstances, I might have chosen the storm. But we can't risk it. Pirates can be fought off, but lightning and gale winds are formidable foes, not to be turned aside with cannon and pistol.

"Head below," I tell the cabin boy. "Help Cook in the galley."

He nods and scurries off. I grip the railing, cursing the storm, cursing the usurper would-be king, cursing every second we can't afford to lose, slipping through the hourglass.

After a moment, I stride to the wheel and take it back from William. My navigator calls out the direction, and I turn the polished mahogany until we're on the new course. Above us, the envelope of the dirigible ponderously follows the rotation. Airships aren't the most graceful of creatures, even smaller ones like the Minotaur.

Another gust from the nearby storm lashes us, but we're already moving away from that particular danger. I give the wheel back to William.

"Everyone, check your pistols," I call. "Gunners, make ready."

"Aye, captain." The powder monkeys scramble below to prepare the cannons.

If we encounter pirates—and given our run of luck lately, it's highly likely—our best defense is to blow a hole in their dirigible canopy. They'll be more careful with us, not wanting to sink their prize, so we'll have the advantage.

But if we miss, they'll be on us like ants on sugar cubes.

With the storm wind at our back, we soon see a smear of land off the starboard bow. Spain. I pull my bronze spyglass from my belt and train it along the coast. Nothing so far, but the pirates have small, fast airships, and lurk where the currents can carry them quickly through the sky.

"Are we safe?" The cabin boy is at my shoulder again, young face anxious as he looks toward the coast.

"No."

He swallows, and glances at the cargo. "Will we reach London before the new king is crowned?"

"I've sworn to do so, or die trying. The last thing England needs is that monster on the throne."

"He's not so bad as that, is he?" The cabin boy's eyes are fringed with ridiculously full lashes. I resist the urge to rub a smudge of dirt off his cheek.

Though English by birth, he's lived a sheltered life on a small Portuguese island, and probably hasn't heard the stories.

"Bad enough," I say. "When he was a boy, the would-be king used to torture the palace dogs. Word has it he's moved on to bigger prey."

"What, horses?"

"People," I say shortly. "Urchins, culled from the slums. Prisoners. Whores."

It's not pretty, but it's the truth. The boy blanches, then gathers himself.

"Then we'd best make good time, captain."

"How's the galley?" I want him below, out of harm's way.

"Cook sent me away because I was whittling at the edge of the table."

I glance at his knife, a serviceable blade, and sharp enough. "Keep that close, and if there's fighting keep your head down."

"I know how to use a knife," he says.

"That may be—but I want you to stay clear of any fights." I study the stubborn lift of his small chin for a moment, thinking of where to send him. "Go down and tell the gun crews to stand by. When they start shooting the cannons, you'll return to the galley."

Cook had better keep the lad out of trouble, or I'll have his bald head.

"Aye, captain."

The cabin boy disappears down the hatch, and I lift my spyglass to my eye again. Movement catches my attention, and I focus the glass.

Damnation.

Not one airship, but two, moving on a course to intercept. I can't see their colors from this distance but I've no doubt they're flying the Jolly Roger.

Pulse ticking up, I glance to port, where the storm crouches and rumbles.

"Ships!" my lookout, Carthy, calls from the rigging.

"I see them."

We can't outrun them, we can't avoid them. Which means we'll have to fight them.

The air feels charged and heavy. The Minotaur continues on her pace, seeming to plod through the air, while ahead the pirates separate, preparing to catch us between them.

Close, closer, and now I can clearly see the skull and crossbones grinning at me from the rigging beneath the sky-blue dirigibles.

"Gunners, make ready!" I call.

The scrape of the cannons being slid forward in the gun ports vibrates the deck. We have three guns, and plenty of powder and balls.

If the pirates close with us, that won't matter.

"On my mark."

I peer through the glass, judging the distance to the ships. As if he can feel my gaze, a bearded man in a bright blue coat lifts his hand in a jaunty wave.

"Azul," I mutter under my breath. We've clashed before.

"Ready." I close up the spyglass with a snap and tuck it back into my belt.

"Aim." I stride back to the wheel, giving William a sharp nod.

He knows what that means. He gives me the wheel, then hurries below to fetch our secret weapon.

Gripping the wheel's handles, I haul the ship over. The rigging creaks as the Minotaur turns, the hull swinging out beneath it. I pray we're close enough.

"Fire!" I yell.

The air erupts with explosions, the dust of gunpowder tangy on my tongue. I watch the balls fly through the sky, just missing Azul's ship. They arc and plummet down, their splashes lost in the sea far below.

"Again!"

I can hear the gunners reloading, and pray that Cook is keeping the newest member of the crew safe in the galley.

A flash of light erupts from the side of Azul's ship. I know what that means.

"Brace yourselves!" I yell, even as Carthy shouts "Incoming!" from above.

One ball goes wide. I hear it hiss past the ship, but the second strikes our hull with a dull thud. Luckily, the reinforced metal sheathing holds—but it won't at close range.

Azul only has two guns, but the pirates have the advantage of maneuverability—not to mention outnumbering us.

"Beware port!" Carthy sings out, and I take my eyes off Azul's ship to see the other vessel is advancing quickly upon us.

I ring the bell beside the wheel twice to notify the crew to hold on, then heel it over hard. Dials whir as the steam-powered propellers adjust, turning the Minotaur about.

Despite our newly outfitted secondary steam engine, we're ponderously slow. *Turn, blast you.* Feet planted on the deck, I grip the wheel hard. We've got to get our cannons facing the second airship.

"Gunners ready?" I call.

"Aye," comes the chorus from below.

"As soon as the other ship's in sight, fire!"

We've no time to waste with the formalities of a captain's countdown. I trust my crew to shoot as soon as the target is available.

Another detonation from Azul's airship, and a second set of cannon balls blasts toward the Minotaur. One thuds into the hull again, and the other arcs higher, crashing through the deck railing before plummeting to the sea. Too close.

Then our guns explode, firing at the second ship. I whip my spyglass up, grinning as I see the hole punctured in their deck. William hastens to my side, carrying a large case. He takes the wheel while I quickly unpack the weapon.

Thunderlash.

It's half gun, half strange device, with bronze protrusions and a crank lever that must be primed before firing. Under strictest confidence, we were given this prototype to bring with us on our mission. It has never been fully tested, and only contains two charges. I hope it doesn't malfunction.

Heeding the inventor's careful instructions, I assemble the weapon and crank back the priming lever. The firing gauge shows ready.

I jam the ear protection on over my close-fitting leather helmet, telescope the machine's legs out front for support, and brace the contraption on my shoulder. Closing one eye, I peer through the sights, swiveling Thunderlash until the sky-blue fabric of the pirate ship's dirigible fills the scope.

Deep breath in. Prepare to fire. I widen my stance. It's a stretch to reach the trigger, but I do, and give it a gentle squeeze.

Boom!

Despite my preparations, I stagger back, shoulder aching from the recoil. The barrel emits wisps of steam as I lower it to the deck. Everything is strangely muffled, until I remember to strip off the headgear.

Cries of consternation echo from the enemy ship. They're losing altitude, the gaping hole in their balloon letting too much helium escape. They toss a few things overboard, but it's a halfhearted attempt at ballast. Already several meters below us, the airship turns tail, making for the coast.

"Well done!" William cries, but his smile of victory fades at the crash of splintering wood.

Azul's ship is close enough now to puncture our hull. And our guns are facing the wrong direction to return fire. Even if we turned, we're too slow, and he'd no doubt dance around us, keeping out of sight of the cannons.

"Surrender!"

I glance at the deck of the pirate ship, to see Azul holding a bullhorn to his lips.

"We promise to treat you gently," he adds.

Even at this distance we can hear the pirate crew's laughter.

"Pretend to agree?" my first mate asks.

"He'd never believe it." I put my hands on my hips and glance down at Thunderlash. The weapon is resetting, but the readiness gauge still shows only half full. "But I might buy us some time."

I stride to the railing. Of course I'm not going to make any promises—a naval airship captain's word cannot be lightly broken—but Azul is fond of his own witticisms. If I can keep him talking for a few precious minutes, we have a chance to bring him down. Quite literally.

"What do you mean by *gently*?" I call.

"Ah, Captain Fury. I look forward to teaching you the meaning. In my bed."

Again the raucous laughter of his crew, but I play along.

"I prefer my men a bit more on the rowdy side," I reply. "Perhaps your first mate might oblige."

Said mate lifts his hook and shakes it at me. We are drawing near enough that I can see the scowl on the man's face.

"Percent?" I ask William in a low voice.

"Nearly there," he says. "Ninety-seven."

I saunter back toward the wheel, deliberately swaying my hips. Usually I downplay the fact that I'm a woman, but at times it can prove useful. In this case, Azul and his men seem distracted enough that when I swoop and pick up Thunderlash, it takes them a moment to react.

That moment gives me time to sight, to prime, to brace...

A high-pitched keening comes from the weapon. I pull it from my shoulder to see the gauge fluctuating wildly. The metal feels hot under my gloved hands.

"Captain!" William cries. "It's going to blow!"

He's right. I lunge toward the railing and, with a searing stab of regret, pitch Thunderlash overboard.

I waited a second too long. The weapon explodes, rocking the Minotaur back and blowing out a section of the deck. I fall to my knees, ears ringing, eyes light-burned. But there's no time.

Captain Azul has seized his chance, and his airship is whirring toward us. His men line the railing, grappling hooks at the ready.

"Sound the alarm!" Carthy cries from the rigging.

The air stinks of scorched metal and vapor. Coughing, I rise and unholster my pistol, sparing a moment's thought for Cook and our newest crew member. Pray they remain safe below.

The clang of the alarm mixes with shouts as the pirates draw alongside.

"Keep them off," I command, striding forward.

The crack of a rifle sounds from overhead—Carthy at his post. One of the pirates tumbles down, a flightless bird lost from the nest. But there are more where he came from. They fling their hooks and, despite my crew's efforts, too many of them catch our railing.

My crew does their best to cut them off, but the fire from the pirates is ferocious. A young ensign goes down to a pistol shot, and I wince. But now's not the time to mourn. That bitter burden comes later.

"Pull to," Captain Azul bellows.

Even as some of his men fall, the rest heave on the ropes. The Minotaur shudders as its balloon bumps the pirate airship's. The gap between the enemy ship and ours narrows. I can see Azul's fierce smile.

Damnation.

The first pirate leaps, dangles a moment from the railing, and is thrown off by my men. His scream fades as he falls. Overhead, Carthy's rifle still cracks out, but the fighting's about to become close quarters. I check my sword—a slim rapier, sharp enough to disembowel a man.

Then there's no time for plans, or regrets. More than a dozen pirates swarm our decks, and I charge in, rapier drawn, knife in my off hand. I search for Azul, but he's keeping behind his men. I do the same, though there's plenty of fighting to go around.

A smelly pirate charges me, his rank odor enough of an advance warning that I pivot to the side, then pull my blade across his throat.

Another pirate shoulders through the fray, his blade sweeping back and forth.

"Captain!" Carthy cries.

I look up, to see him pointing at the hatch. Whirling, I spot a red-capped pirate descending. Heart leaping like a hare, I sprint to the hatch and fling myself down the stairs. A cry comes from the galley.

No!

At the galley door, I halt at the pool of blood spreading over the planks. I make myself look inside. The cabin boy stands there, knife still dripping. Beside him, Cook holds a bloodied cleaver. The pirate's dead body lies on the floor before them.

Thank the heavens.

"Well done," I gasp, then whirl and hurry back to the fighting.

I arrive on deck to hear Captain Azul bellowing. As quickly as they boarded, the pirates flee back to their ship, leaving their dead and wounded behind. The freshly-scrubbed boards are stained with new blood, and I make a quick tally. I've lost three men, the pirates a half dozen.

With their second airship disabled, they were outnumbered from the start, but their retreat is too abrupt. I see Azul glance into the sky behind me, and then motion his men for more haste. The pirates abandon their grapples and pile back onto their ship, which is already pulling away.

One hapless man dangles from a hastily reclaimed grapple rope, his legs kicking in the air as the smaller ship picks up speed.

The back of my neck prickling, I slowly turn, dread knowledge of what I'll see freezing my blood.

The Sky Kraken.

Like some horrible, misshapen airship, the bulbous balloon of its body rises in the air. Its long tentacles whip about and its slitted eye fixes upon the Minotaur with an evil gleam. Belching out sulphurous fumes, it propels itself forward in spurts of odorous gases. Seen from afar, its manner of locomotion might appear humorous, but there's nothing remotely funny about the monster bearing down upon us.

"Fly!" I scream.

Gouts of steam erupt from the engine room. It won't be enough.

I motion at Carthy in the rigging. "Deploy the sails," I call. "Hands aloft!"

We have the small blessing of a following wind. Glancing at the silken sails already billowing out, I hurry to the hatch.

The dimness below decks enfolds me again, along with the smell of coal smoke. I stride down to the engine room, passing the galley. As I go, the cabin boy steps out and follows me.

"Is the battle over?" he asks.

"The pirates are gone, but we've a worse enemy on our tail." I glance over my shoulder at him. "You know where the parachutes are stowed?"

His eyes widen, but he gives me a determined nod. "Will it come to that, Captain Fury? Abandoning the ship?"

"It might." I hate to admit it. "But I won't abandon you. You've my word on that. None of this going down with my ship business."

At least, not this time.

We reach the engine room, the heat already making perspiration spring up beneath my leather helmet.

"Can we get more speed?" I ask the engineer, though I know the crew's doing their best.

"Coal won't burn any hotter," she says.

Right. Maybe it needs a little more encouragement—and we need to lighten our load.

"Run up top," I tell the cabin boy. "Tell the men to start bringing the brandy down. And don't stare too long at the beast."

"The... beast?"

I nod. He swallows, once, then hurries away toward the hatch. Good, tough material there. He'll do well, once he gets his legs under him. And I suppose it will do him good to see the Sky Kraken. Not many can claim to have set eyes on the beast and lived.

"Throw the brandy on the fire when it arrives," I tell my engineer, then hold up my hand when she opens her mouth. "I know the tolerances won't allow for it—but dammit, we have to move faster."

She closes his mouth. "Aye, captain."

"I trust you to make the necessary repairs and adjustments to keep us running ahead of the Sky Kraken."

She pales at this information, but her expression is determined. There'll be bonuses all around, if I can bring the Minotaur safely to port.

As I head back to the deck, a string of crewmen carrying bottles of brandy pass me. Clever thought, to break open the crates. Faster than lugging the ungainly boxes below. I wonder if it was the cabin boy's idea.

I take a deep breath as I emerge on deck, then regret it as the tang of sulphur fills my nose. The beast lashes its tentacles through the air behind us. It's gaining.

The ocean winks, blue and untroubled, below. I stride to the fore railing and pull out my spyglass. Twisting the brass, I squint at the haze on the horizon ahead. Could be fog, but I pray it's England. Once land is in sight, the air patrols should come to our aid.

If we make it that far.

The airship bucks a little, then surges forward. I smile grimly. A shame to waste all that good brandy, but worse to waste our lives.

I join the cabin boy at the railing, where he's staring at the Sky Kraken. It bobs up and down, its triangular mouth snapping as though eager for a taste of blood. The tentacles whip out, in, out. I judge another few minutes and it will be close enough to latch on to our ship.

"A rather gruesome sight," I say.

"Horrid." The cabin boy shivers. "What if it catches us?"

"Then you prepare to leap overboard."

The ship lurches again, and he stumbles. I catch the back of his coat to steady him, then hand him the spyglass.

"Look ahead for land," I say. The lad needs something to distract him from the bloated, belching death at our heels.

After a few moments, the cabin boy takes the glass from his eye.

"I think I see it. Is that England?" His pale hand trembles a little as he returns my spyglass.

I twist the bronze fittings, and can't help letting out a breath of relief. "Aye, that's England. And those specks are royal naval airships. As soon as they spot us, they'll come to our rescue."

Provided the monster doesn't catch us first.

As if realizing its quarry might escape, the Sky Kraken lets out an enormous emission and scoots forward. It lashes a tentacle out, and more of my beleaguered deck railing shatters under the blow.

"More speed!" I yell, not that it will do any good.

If only I had the Thunderlash.

There's no point in coming about and trying to shoot the monster with our cannons—by then it will be upon us, ripping the ship to pieces.

Carthy's shooting again from the rigging, but I doubt the

rifle will do more than annoy the beast. The only thing we can do is stay in the air, and bring the monster close enough for our sister ships to fire upon.

The Sky Kraken whips another tentacle at us, this time snagging one of the sails and ripping it down. It brings the length of cloth to its sharp mouth, then spits it out again. Then, thank heavens, the Minotaur lurches forward again. I pray we have enough brandy to propel us to the coast.

The beast lashes at us again. Misses. It lets out a bellow of rage.

"Sound the alarm," I cry.

The bell clangs out, and the Sky Kraken falters, just for a moment. Is it susceptible to sound?

"Ready the guns!" I turn to the cabin boy. "Run down and tell the gunners to fire as soon as the cannons are loaded and primed."

"What target?"

"Nothing—they don't even have to put shot in. We just need to make as much of a racket as possible. Then tell Cook to come up here with some pots and spoons. Go —quickly!"

He sprints away, and I bite my lip and watch the Sky Kraken swim closer. With another sulphurous gust it surges forward. This time, instead of lashing about, it slides its tentacles forward. The seeking tips brush the hull, and then adhere.

"Hold fast!" I yell, glancing at the lads in the rigging.

Carthy fires, and hits one of the tentacles. The Sky Kraken takes no notice, despite the green ichor seeping from the wound.

Then it pulls, and the Minotaur's deck tilts. I skid toward

the railing, hit the wood hard and hold on. Slowly, our airship is being reeled in toward the beast.

Not a moment too soon, the cannons fire. The Sky Kraken jerks, releasing the Minotaur. We swing forward, and I smell brandy fumes as the engineers throw more spirits on the coal.

I regain my footing and stride to the alarm bell, and Cook and the cabin boy emerge from the hatch, bearing steel pots and spoons.

"Good," I say. "Make as much noise as possible."

I ring the alarm bell, my first mate grabs an extra pot and spoon, and we set to making a colossal racket. The guns go off sporadically, Carthy fires from the rigging, and on the whole we produce quite the clamor.

It's not enough to deter the beast from following us. Instead of reaching its tentacles out, though, it seems bent on overtaking us—probably so that it can crush us in one blow, and put an end to our aural assault.

Despite the brandy and our desperate pot-banging, the Sky Kraken draws ever nearer. Its malevolent eye swivels, seeming to fix directly upon me, and I suppress a shudder.

The stinking balloon of its body quivers. Slowly, it raises half of its dozen tentacles. They reach up into the cloudless blue, up, and up. When they descend, they will crack our hull in two.

"To the parachutes!" I cry. This is the end.

I send a last glance at the dark mass of England looming ahead, and swallow back the taste of failure. So close.

The tentacles shiver with anticipation. I haul the cabin boy by his coat to the parachutes and thrust one at him.

Then the air around us explodes as the HMS Hydra

descends from above, guns blazing. They hit the Sky Kraken's body, and it lets out a high-pitched shriek that grates like metal in my ears.

Abruptly, it sucks its tentacles back, tucks them beneath its body, and careens down and away. A trail of greenish smoke follows in its wake.

My men set up a cheer, and I clap Cook and the cabin boy on the back.

"Well done," I say, relief nearly choking me.

"Is the monster gone?" The lad peers over the railing. "Is it dead?"

"Not dead, I'm sure—but wounded and gone to whatever dreadful place it claims for its lair."

"Then we're safe?"

"I believe so. Now, we must make London before sundown." Already the sun is sliding toward the horizon.

"Ahoy the Minotaur!" the captain of the Hydra hails us, the warship coming to float alongside. "Is all well?"

"Thank you for the timely intervention," I say. "We're well enough, all told."

He doesn't need to hear about the pirates.

"Never thought I'd clap eyes on that dreadful beast," he says. "Quite the show. May we escort you to London port?"

"To London, yes." I judge the angle of the sun. "However, we must make directly for the palace."

He nods, the plume in his hat bobbing. "Lead on."

With the dint of the rest of the brandy and our backup sails we make good time to London. The Thames is a silver ribbon below, and the city is beautiful to my eyes, even hazed with soot and steam. Church towers and the cathedral dome catch the last of the light, gilded gold, as we drop anchor directly above Buckingham Palace. A group of sympathetic soldiers wait below. At least, I hope they're sympathetic.

"Ready the ropes and harness," I call.

My riggers scramble, and soon myself, my first mate, and the cabin boy are ready to descend. On the ground, the soldiers have caught the ends of the ropes and tied them to anchor points.

"Come behind me," I tell the lad. "If you slip, I'll catch you."

He nods, pale-faced and determined.

I clip myself to the rope, make sure the brake catches, then step backwards over the railing. As I kick off from the ship, the harness tightens about my legs and chest. For a moment I free fall, taking in the glorious sight of the city, the sun burning on the horizon. Then I brake, jolting myself to a more manageable speed. My teeth are cold from grinning so widely into the wind.

"Ready," I cry, and feel the cabin boy attach to the rope.

He slides down less recklessly than I, but maintains a reasonable speed. We approach the manicured hedges, and the soldiers rush up to assist. I land, catch my balance, and quickly unharness.

William arrives seconds later, and we're both ready and waiting by the time the cabin boy reaches the ground.

"Quickly," I say to the soldiers, "take us to the throne room."

The redcoats break into a trot, leading us through a side door into the opulent hallways of the palace. The marble floors ring with the sound of our boot heels, and I catch quick glimpses of our party in the gilt-framed mirrors lining the hall.

A blur of scarlet. A small, dark-haired airship captain. An equally petite cabin boy, soot smudged across one cheek, fear and resolve shining in equal measure from his face.

"Here we are, sir." The lead soldier throws open an ornately carved door.

We tumble inside the large room. I take in the sight of a tall, thin-nosed man seated with an ermine-lined cloak about his shoulders. Egbert, the would-be king.

Before him stands the Archbishop of Canterbury, the crown of England in his upraised hands.

"Stop!" I shout.

The crowd turns to stare at us in consternation.

"Seize these interlopers," Egbert says.

A group of soldiers move toward us, but I ignore them. Taking the cabin boy by the arm, I thrust forward, pushing aside velvet-clad nobles and perfumed ladies.

The soldiers who met us upon the lawn follow close behind, forming a wall between us and Egbert's men. I tow the cabin boy to the dais where Egbert sits.

"I demand you step down," I say. "You are a usurper, not fit to sit upon the throne."

The nobles gasp, and Egbert regards me coldly.

"Who are you, to impugn me, the only heir?"

"I'm Captain Jane Fury of HMS Minotaur, but that's not important." I pull the cabin boy in front of me. "I have with me the *real* heir to the throne, and the next monarch of England. Ladies and gentlemen, may I introduce Olivia Charlotte Waite-Hanover, daughter of the late king and queen, spirited away to be raised in secrecy, and safety, on a Portuguese island."

The room fills with excited conversation as the word

spreads. Egbert is not a popular man. Feared, yes. Despised, indeed. Given no other alternative, the people of England were forced to accept him as their ruler. Luckily, there is now another choice.

"Lies!" Egbert rises, his expression furious. "This is clearly an imposter."

"I invite you to put her to whatever tests you feel necessary," I say. "However, the new science of heredity has confirmed that Lady Olivia is who she claims to be. We have proof positive that this young woman is the true heir. I swear it, upon my word as a captain in the Royal Airship Navy."

There have long been rumors of a hidden heir, but England had given up hope—until the stunning truth of Lady Olivia's existence was revealed, and I was sent on the top-secret mission to retrieve her.

"I am so sorry, my lord," the archbishop says to Egbert, laying the crown back on its red velvet cushion. "Please remove the cloak and step aside."

"I...but...this is outrageous," Egbert sputters.

Two of my retinue of soldiers step forward. Reluctantly, the former heir strips off the cloak and tosses it back upon the wooden throne.

"I won't forget this, Captain Fury," he says, eyes narrowed.

"Good." Better that I'm the target of his anger than the new queen.

"My lady." The archbishop bows to my young companion.

With a dignity beyond her eighteen years, Lady Olivia Charlotte Waite-Hanover steps forward, accepts the mantle of rulership, and seats herself upon the throne.

As the crown settles upon her head, the crowd lets out a cheer.

"Long live the queen!"

Indeed. England has been saved, and my former cabin boy has the makings of an excellent queen. If storms, pirates, and the Sky Kraken could not make her quail, she can surely navigate the turbulent waters ahead. I catch her eye and grin, then raise my gloved fists in victory.

"For Her Majesty, Queen Olivia!" I cry. "Long may she reign!"

THE SUN NEVER SETS

London, 1850

S even degrees above the horizon, she spotted it—a speck of diamond in the deepening twilight. A tiny dot of light that perchance was only a trick of vision, or a wayward dust mote.

But perhaps something more...

Miss Kate Danville's heart raced at the prospect, but she forced herself to remain still. With a deep, steadying breath, she leaned forward and gently twisted the eyepiece of her telescope, careful not to bump the instrument. The pinprick of brightness lost focus, then sharpened.

She was not mistaken. Certainty flared through her, filling her with warmth.

The image blurred again, but this time due to her own triumphant tears. Kate sat back and brushed the foolish water from her eyes. She would show them all that her *little hobby* as Father called it—Mother used stronger words like *unsuitable* and *distastefully unfeminine*—was more than simply dabbling in the astronomical arts.

She, Miss Kate Danville, had discovered a comet!

Oh, she was not the first women to do so—a handful of amateur astronomers had been the first to spot celestial objects, including her idol, Maria Mitchell, who received the Danish gold medal just two years prior.

Kate closed her eyes and imagined the King of Denmark presenting her with that accolade in front of an admiring crowd. Why, she might even get to meet the esteemed Ms. Mitchell, and perhaps be inducted into the Royal Society—

"Beg pardon, miss, but her ladyship sent me up to fetch you to make ready for the ball." The maid's reedy voice broke through Kate's daydream, bringing her down from the stars with a thud.

She opened her eyes, and was once again simply Miss Kate Danville, perched on the top of Danville House with her telescope and her fancies in the sooty June dusk.

"I need a bit more time," she told the maid. "Please tell my mother I must notate my new discovery."

The maid gave her a skeptical look, but dropped a curtsy. "I shall, but you know Lady Danville won't take kindly to that answer."

"I am well aware of my mother's expectations." They included a proper marriage and Kate's abandoning her inappropriate scientifical leanings.

But that disapproval would surely change once Kate's Comet was officially recognized.

Time was of the essence, however. Kate bent again to her telescope to jot down the exact location of the bright speck in the sky. If someone else notified the Royal Astronomical

Society first, she would be robbed of her discovery. That must *not* be allowed to happen.

"Kate!" Her mother's sharp tones drifted up from the stairwell leading to the attic. "If you don't come down this instant, I declare I will have your father take your telescope away."

Lady Danville would never attempt to navigate the steep stairs—neither her wide skirts nor her temperament would allow the journey—but she was not averse to raising her voice. Or delivering threats.

"Coming," Kate called.

She hastily scribbled a second set of notes, then tucked the precious piece of paper into her pocket. Time to face her mother, and yet another social tedium where the gentlemen asked her whether she liked roses, or droned on about their own accomplishments.

She blew out an unhappy breath. Lady Danville was determined to see Kate betrothed by the end of the summer, while Kate was equally determined to resist.

Although, upon further consideration, attending the ball that evening might be for the best. If Viscount Huffton or one of the other Royal Society astronomers were there, she could notify them of her discovery at once.

AT BREAKFAST TWO DAYS LATER, Kate stared at the morning headline in the *London Times*. Shock stole her breath and held her motionless for a heartbeat.

"Viscount Huffton Discovers New Comet," the paper declared.

No. That weasel had taken credit for her discovery!

"I won't stand for it," she gasped, leaping to her feet and nearly overturning the teapot. "I must pay a call upon Lord Wrottesley at once."

Surely, as one of the founding members of the Royal Astronomical Society, he would aid her. She knew he was in London, for the odious Viscount Huffton had mentioned it at the ball. The ball where he had stolen the fruits of her labors. Her hands clenched into fists.

"Sit down," her mother said, regarding her sternly over the white damask tablecloth. "What an unladylike outburst. And you have never been introduced to Lord Wrottesley. You cannot simply visit the man—what would he think of such improper behavior?"

Kate slowly sank back into her chair and used her napkin to mop up the spilled tea. "Please, mother. It's important."

Thank heavens she'd kept her original notes. She only prayed Lord Wrottesley would listen when she explained that *she* had spotted the comet first, then brought her findings to the viscount. Who was supposed to have reported it to the Royal Society, not claimed the discovery as his own, the worm.

Lady Danville raised her brows. "Is this matter important enough that you will consent to receive Lord Downing-Wilton tomorrow, should he pay you a visit?"

Oh, rot it. Kate should have known her mother would take every opportunity to foist a suitor upon her. She closed her eyes a moment, pushing back the scream of frustration bubbling in her throat. When she had mastered herself, she opened her eyes.

"Of course, mother. Only, we must see Lord Wrottesley today."

"So you keep insisting." Lady Danville regarded her a moment more. "It is most irregular. Perhaps you ought to admit Sir Wexfield into your circle, as well."

"As you say." Kate spoke the words through gritted teeth.

"And perhaps—"

"I shall go up and change now." Kate tossed the tea-stained napkin upon the table. She had lost her appetite completely.

"Wear your dove walking dress with the violet trim," her mother said. "If we are fortunate, Lord Wrottesley will be entertaining gentleman guests when we arrive."

As it transpired, and to Kate's great relief, Lord Wrottesley was at home, and he was alone. The butler ushered them into his cluttered study, where Kate presented her notes and explained the circumstances.

"Hmph." Lord Wrottesley peered at the jotted numbers and angles, then shook his head. "That puppy Huffton needs to be taken down a peg. Thank you for bringing this to my attention, Miss Danville."

Kate slid forward to the edge of her chair. "Does this mean my claim will be upheld?"

Lady Danville, seated in the adjoining wingback, gave her a placid smile. "Patience, my dear. I'm certain Lord Wrottesley does not like to be rushed. He will do what is best."

"But—"

"Thank you, sir, for your time." Lady Danville rose. "Certainly you have more pressing concerns than listening to my daughter complain."

"Perhaps." He folded Kate's notes and tapped them against his hand. "I shall review the evidence and share it with the Royal Astronomical Society. Thank you for your visit, ladies."

Before Kate could protest, her mother hauled her to the doorway. She dropped a quick curtsey to Lord Wrottesley, and then the butler shut the study door in her face.

KATE SPENT a wretched two days being polite, if not pleasant, to a stream of gentleman callers. None of them were the least bit interested in discussing any type of science, let alone astronomy, and several of them looked faintly horrified that she would broach the subject at all.

It was worth it, though, when she received the letter bearing the seal of the Royal Society, confirming that she, Kate Danville, was credited with the discovery of what would henceforth be known as Miss Danville's Comet.

Throughout the following week, the mote in the sky grew brighter. First it matched, then overtook, the light of the stars, until it was visible during the day as well as searing the night. Her comet went from being a source of mild speculation to casting a worrisome light over the population of London. Reports soon came in that the comet was affecting every corner of the British Empire.

Local uprisings, raving prophets, and strange tides were reported regularly in the newspapers, along with sensationalized speculation: the comet would smash into London and devastate the country—nay, the entire world, it was not a comet at all but a vehicle bearing explorers from the stars, the end times were nigh and everyone might as well drink and make merry while they still could. Some took this as a call to rampage about the streets, causing an increasing number of clashes between unruly members of the populace and the constabulary.

Queen Victoria issued a half dozen regal reassurances—none of which were taken to heart. It was noted that she and Prince Albert sent their children up to Scotland with a coterie of Royal Nannies, prompting an exodus of nobly-born sons and daughters to the countryside.

Kate, however, refused to go.

"Mother, I'm seventeen, not a child. And I've been invited to court to speak with the queen on Thursday afternoon. Surely you would not deprive me of such a triumph?"

Social standing won over familial safety, and Kate was allowed to remain in an increasingly turbulent London.

By Wednesday, the Royal Society astronomers confirmed that the celestial object was, indeed, on a trajectory toward London. They were no longer calling it a comet, however, as it was behaving in a rather perplexing—some might say frightening—manner. The astronomer's calculations suggested that the object was under its own power, able to make course and speed adjustments.

Kate had to agree that they appeared to be correct, based on her own observations. In addition, the object grew closer every hour, until it was a looming brightness over the country. Speculation exploded, and apprehension turned to panic as soldiers began to filter into London. The queen exhorted her subjects to remain calm, and expressed her approval of those who chose to carry on with their daily lives.

Handbills were posted at every corner, bearing Queen

Victoria's profile and the words, "Nothing is certain, except that We will meet this Challenge with Fortitude, Grace, and the Might of God and Empire behind Us. Stay strong and true, Loyal Subjects, and fear not."

Kate's original euphoria at discovering the comet had curdled to an odd mix of pride and guilt. In a way, she felt responsible for whatever was about to happen.

If she had not first identified that speck in the sky, would it have changed its course? Had the act of observing its approach made its arrival inevitable? Was the Empire, perhaps the entire earth, doomed?

In a brave attempt at normalcy, the queen and prince continued to keep their court hours at Buckingham Palace. The Prime Minister and most of the peers still in London spent their time cloistered in Parliament, arguing over what course to pursue.

Thursday dawned bright, with the strange metallic light filtering over the city, and the Danville household made ready for Kate's appearance at court.

"Must you tie my laces so tightly?" Kate asked the maid. "I can scarcely breathe."

"Not every day you're invited to the palace, Miss." Still, the woman left off trying to constrict Kate's lungs beyond bearing, and fetched the rose muslin day dress from the wardrobe.

An hour later, appropriately garbed and coiffed and bejeweled, Kate and her mother stepped into their carriage. The footman folded up the steps and closed the door, and the driver set out for the palace. Despite the well-sprung seats, every jolt over the cobblestones sent a jab through Kate. She tried to distract herself by looking out the window, but there was little to be seen. All the fine shops were closed up, and only a few dandies roamed the streets instead of the cream of Society going about their business. Most of the upper crust had departed London for their country estates.

"Will the looting spread this far?" Kate asked her mother.

"Of course not. The rabble knows better than to set foot in Mayfair."

Despite the clipped assurance in Lady Danville's tone, Kate could not help noticing that her mother's gloved fingers were laced tightly together in her lap.

"Do you think Parliament has come up with a plan?"

Lady Danville sniffed. "According to your father, nothing but dithering is being accomplished. At least there are plenty of soldiers about. Don't fret, darling. Everything shall turn out for the best. I have utmost faith in the queen."

Kate was not convinced the queen could, by pure force of royal will, keep a meteor from smashing London to smithereens. Yet what else could they do but persevere?

The approach to Buckingham Palace was crowded with people. Some were shouting for the queen and God to save them, some were exhorting the throng to rush the gates, while others held signs proclaiming the world's imminent destruction. Overhead, the bright sphere in the sky appeared to be growing larger.

With the aid of a dozen red-coated soldiers, the carriage managed to push past the press of bodies and through the well-guarded iron gates of the palace. Behind them, Kate heard the crowd murmuring like a restless creature ready to leap from its kennel.

A shout and the crack of a gunshot made both Kate and

her mother jump. Kate's heartbeat thudded in her chest, and Lady Danville pushed open the window.

"What is happening?" she demanded, her voice shrill.

A soldier jumped up, catching the side of the carriage, and the vehicle rocked slightly from his weight.

"Rest easy, ladies," he said. "The rabble tried to rush forward, but so far shots fired into the air are keeping them back. We'll have you to the door in a trice."

Lady Danville nodded at him, then patted nervously at her hair. The gates shut behind them with a clang that Kate did not find as reassuring as she ought.

Their driver pulled the carriage up before the arched entry, and the footman handed Lady Danville and Kate out. Guards stood impassively on either side of the doors, ignoring the strange light overhead and the cries of the crowd.

A liveried servant waiting before the entryway glanced at the crest on their carriage, then bowed to Kate's mother.

"Lady Danville, Miss Danville, you are expected. Please, follow me."

He led them into the palace, past the grand sweeping double staircase and down a high-ceilinged hall lined with paintings and the marble busts of former rulers. The air smelled of flowers and lemon polish, with an undertone of must.

Kate lifted her chin and resolved to remain calm. Although her mother thought the queen only wanted to congratulate her on her discovery, Kate feared an interrogation lay ahead.

The servant ushered them through a set of tall doors and into an immense room decorated in scarlet and white. The numerous soldiers scattered about the hall looked as though they had been placed there for decoration, in their matching red and white. The ceiling overhead was ornately patterned, but the most imposing sight was at the far end, where Queen Victoria sat upon an elaborately carved and gilt-covered throne.

A crown set with rubies adorned her brown hair, and her large, dark eyes surveyed the hall from above her thin nose and rounded cheeks. At her side sat Prince Albert, dressed in a military uniform. He was slighter than Kate had anticipated—or perhaps he was simply dwarfed by the queen's voluminous indigo skirts and penetrating gaze.

The room was filled with nobility: lords looking somber and consulting their pocket watches, ladies whose laughter sounded a bit too forced, a handful of young bucks who turned and watched the Danville ladies enter with over-bright eyes.

And a cluster of Royal Society astronomers, including Lord Wrottesley and the contemptible Viscount Huffton. Kate deliberately glared at the man, hoping the viscount would feel the burn of her stare, unmannered though it might be.

"Wait here," the servant said, leading Kate and her mother to the side of the room. "The steward will fetch you when the queen is ready."

"Very good," Lady Danville said, then turned to her daughter. "Kate, you must remember to smile. And don't, I pray, speak overmuch. The queen has far more important matters to attend to than listening to you drone on about telescopes."

Kate swallowed past the dryness in her throat.

"Yes, mother," she said.

In truth, she could not offer the queen any better insight than the astronomers. Despite watching the approaching object every night, she had gleaned no particular truths or insights from it—other than it appeared to be headed on a direct trajectory toward London, and approaching rapidly.

An officious-looking fellow wearing the palace livery and an ornate medallion about his neck, strutted up to them.

"Miss Danville, the queen will speak with you now."

Kate smoothed the pink flounces on her skirt and tried to calm her sudden surge of nerves.

"Well, come along," her mother said. "We mustn't keep her majesty waiting."

The steward turned a cold eye on Lady Danville. "You may remain here, madam. The queen wishes to converse with your daughter, not you."

Lady Danville's mouth hung open for a moment. She snapped it shut, a flush creeping up from her neck.

"Very well," she said with a sniff. "Kate, pray endeavor not to embarrass the family name."

There was really no response Kate could make to that. She gave her mother a tight smile, then let the steward usher her through the room. Whispers followed in their wake, a buzz of gossip hovering like gnats about her head. As they passed the knot of astronomers, Lord Wrottesley gave her an encouraging nod, while Viscount Huffton looked bitter.

"Miss Kate Danville," the steward announced when they were before the thrones.

Kate bowed her head and dipped into her best curtsey, her heart pounding so loudly she feared the queen could hear it.

"Rise," Queen Victoria said, beckoning her to approach. "Welcome to court, Miss Danville. I understand you were the first to spot the object now approaching London.?"

"Yes, your majesty." With force of will, Kate kept her fingers from knotting desperately together.

Prince Albert gave her a sharp look. "Indeed. Do tell us more. Do you have any idea what it is?"

"I'm simply an amateur astronomer, your highness. I don't—"

"Your majesty!" A guard burst into the room and ran up to the thrones, halting a few paces away to make a breathless bow.

"Yes?" the queen asked, her tone unbelievably calm.

"The thing in the sky, it's stopped. And, and..." He gulped for breath.

"Out with it, man," the price snapped.

"Something has detached from it, and is approaching through the sky."

A buzz of speculation moved through the room, edged with panic. Kate bit her lip.

"Approaching through the sky, you say?" The queen rose, her skirts rustling. "Well then. We had best repair to the palace gardens to better view whatever is transpiring."

"My dear." The prince caught her arm. "Do you think it's safe?"

Queen Victoria gave him a quelling look. "I am Queen of England, Princess of Hanover, Empress of India and supreme monarch of the British Empire. I shall not cower inside while great events unfold at my doorstep. And if we are all to perish, let it be said that we went forth to meet our fate bravely."

"Of course." Price Albert gave her a faint smile. "Lead on, my lady."

The queen, the prince, and their guards swept forward. Half of the court went with them, including the astronomers, while the rest clearly did not want to risk setting foot outside the dubious safety of the palace.

Kate followed close behind, her pulse racing with fear and anticipation. *Something* was finally happening, and she, Miss Kate Danville, was about to witness a great event in history.

As they traversed the hallways and formal rooms of Buckingham Palace, Kate did not try to locate her mother in the throng. Lady Danville could hang safely back, or attempt to return home, but Kate resolved to remain as close to the center of events as possible.

Even though it might prove her doom.

Yet the fact that something was approaching—something smaller than the glowing sphere that filled the sky—suggested it was guided by intelligent entities. Perhaps it was simliar to a tender boat being launched out from a great galleon.

What a frightening thought! If that were the case, she could only hope these visitors from the stars were as benign and enlightened as the British explorers who landed upon heathen islands, bringing civilization and enlightenment to the poor natives on faraway shores.

Following that reasoning, then, if there truly *were* beings from beyond the stars, humans would be the ignorant savages. Kate gave a sharp shake of her head. She did not like that notion one bit.

At last they reached several pairs of French doors leading

out to the terraces behind the palace. Outside, the sunshine was overlaid with silver, making the grass and shrubbery appear metallic.

The guards opened a set of doors, then preceded the queen and prince outside. Shading their eyes, they peered upward.

"Good gad," one of the redcoats exclaimed. "It appears to be heading directly for us."

The remainder of the court poured out onto the terrace. The air was filled with a deep, nearly inaudible hum. The light struck Kate like a blow, and she blinked against the brilliance. One of the queen's ladies in waiting handed the monarch a parasol, and a few others sprouted above the throng like colorful mushrooms after a rain.

Lacking that apparatus, Kate cupped her hands around her eyes and squinted into the sky. *Good heavens!* And rather literally, at that.

The shining sphere hung over London, so bright she could not look at it for long. From the sphere, a dark ribbon descended—a plume of smoke left by a smaller orb. That object was most decidedly coming closer.

Was it a weapon, aimed at the heart of the Empire?

"Your majesty," the captain of the guard urged, "please, return inside."

"I will not be any safer within the walls than without," Queen Victoria replied. "Whatever is approaching, we must meet it with fortitude."

Already, the orb was much closer. Kate estimated it would land in the garden in no less than two minutes. As it approached the noise grew to a loud rumble.

The soldiers lifted their guns and trained them on the

dark blot descending from the sky. Closer. Closer, until it was the size of a small outbuilding. It brushed past a few trees on the outskirts of the garden, and their branches snapped off and tumbled to the ground.

The air shook with a deep, mechanical roar. The surface of the man-made lake nearby shivered violently. Kate clapped her hands over her ears, watching as the object slowed to nearly a hover.

With excruciating delicacy, it landed on the manicured lawn of Buckingham Palace. The blades of grass beneath it wilted and sizzled. The orb seemed made of metal, yet no light sheened off the surface, and it had no discernible seams or rivets.

The noise cut off, and for a moment Kate wondered if she'd gone deaf. Perspiration stuck her dress to her chest, and she plucked at the fabric. Then the shouts of approaching soldiers punctuated the air as they poured into the garden and surrounded the black hulk of the orb, raising their guns.

"Hold your fire," the queen commanded, sweeping out one gloved hand.

The soldiers shifted, but remained at the ready.

Noiselessly, the orb split in the front to reveal an elongated oval opening. Something stirred inside. The crowd leaned forward, fearfully fascinated, like a rodent before the sway of a cobra.

Faint movement—and then a creature floated out. It was not human, although it had two long appendages on either side that might be termed arms, and a head on top of its torso, surrounded by a clear bubble. Two flat, black eyes, turned on the crowd. Below those eyes, the creature had a slit for a nose, and a mouth full of writhing tentacles.

Bile rose in Kate's throat at the sight, and she swayed. A nearby lady screamed and fainted, eased to the ground by her companion. No one else bestirred themselves to help— they were all transfixed by the dreadful sight hovering before them.

One of the soldiers yelled and discharged his musket. Kate flinched at the sound, half hoping the bullet hit its mark, the other half knowing they were all doomed.

The creature turned its head, and the soldier slumped to the ground. It was impossible to tell if he were dead, or merely stunned.

"Halt!" Queen Victoria cried, her voice finally taut with fear. "Do not shoot."

"But, your majesty—" the captain of the guard began.

"No. We shall wait, and greet this creature as civilized beings, not vicious animals." The queen took a single step forward. Her grip on her parasol seemed inordinately tight.

The thing turned toward Queen Victoria, and Prince Albert caught her elbow.

"Greetings," the queen called. "We mean you no harm."

"Yet," a nearby lord muttered. "I think we're better off shooting the damned thing."

His wife hushed him, and Kate could not decide if she agreed with the man or not. Part of her could not believe this was happening—that the glint of light she had first spotted two weeks ago had brought a being from the stars to land here, in the heart of London. Such things simply did not happen.

And yet, the dark orb sat implacably on the greensward, and its occupant was even now gliding toward the terrace.

Kate sucked back a breath and resisted the urge to bolt for the French doors and cower beneath a table. Instead she clenched her hands and watched. The creature stopped a safe distance from the queen. Perhaps it understood the tightening of soldiers' fingers on their guns, or recognized the acrid smell of human fear.

A crackling sound filled the air, and then a voice. Inhuman, certainly, with odd inflections and staggered pauses, but the words it spoke were recognizable.

"These...beings wish no harm is speaking...to ruler of earth."

There was a pause, and Kate wondered if the last bit had been meant as a question. The queen seemed to draw the same conclusion.

"Indeed," the queen said. "I am Queen Victoria, ruler of the British Empire. Who are you?"

"We are...eeixlltiey." The final word was a garble of sound. Likely there was no match for it in the English language.

The creature's tentacled mouth did not move, and the voice seemed to emanate more from the orb it had arrived in than from the alien figure. Still, there was no doubt it was communicating directly with them.

"Welcome to earth, Yxleti," the queen said, making a valiant attempt to pronounce the name. "Tell us, why have you come?"

"To observe...explore...assess..."

A bead of sweat ran down the side of Kate's neck, and she wiped it away. She did not much like the idea of being "assessed" by inhuman creatures from the stars. But they had devised a way to communicate in English, and clearly been wise enough to come directly to the queen of the largest empire on earth.

The prince leaned over and whispered something in Queen Victoria's ear. She nodded, then turned to her captain of the guard.

"I believe our further dealings with the Yxleti are best done more privately," she said, in a carrying voice. "Your guards may remain, of course, and my attendents, but please disperse the onlookers."

The group of Royal Society astronomers protested, as did a few self-important lords. The rest of the crowd began to edge back toward the palace. No one quite turned their backs on the creature, or the strange conveyance in which it had arrived.

Kate was torn. Part of her wished nothing more than to find her mother and flee the bizarre spectacle. She craved a hot bath, and the opportunity to forget for as long as possible the proceedings of the afternoon.

Yet a larger part was aquiver with possibility. Their world had changed, of that there could be no question. She had been witness to what could only be the most extraordinary event in human history. She could meekly turn away and return to the path her parents and Society had laid out, or she could seize the opportunity before her. This was her chance.

Lifting her skirts, Kate strode past the astronomers, taking some small satisfaction from treading upon Viscount Huffton's foot.

"Your majesty." She made the queen another curtsey. "I

beg your leave to remain. As discoverer of the vessel that bore this star explorer hither, I will pledge my life to your service, to the Empire, and to forwarding the understanding between humans and Yxleti. Please, let me stay."

The queen regarded her a long moment from her cool brown eyes, and Kate fought to keep her legs from trembling. She must be confident and bold in this moment.

"Miss Kate Danville," the queen said, "are you betrothed?"

"No, your majesty." Despite her mother's best efforts. "I am wholly committed to this endeavor, if you will accept me."

"Your majesty," Lord Wrottesley approached the queen. "If I may speak?"

The queen nodded, and the astronomer continued. "I happen to know that this is a young lady of great fortitude and determination. You might do well to take her."

Queen Victoria inclined her head. "Very good. We consent to add you to our staff—for the time being. You may remain here."

Kate shot a grateful look at Lord Wrottesley. She did not care if he had put in a word for her simply to spite Viscount Huffton, or if he truly believed she had the mettle to be of service. In either case, she vowed to be worthy.

In moments only a small retinue surrounding the queen remained, including the astronomers and her guardsmen. The Yxleti had stayed silent, impassively floating a few handspans above the ground as the humans reorganized themselves.

Kate glanced at the flat black eyes and suppressed a shiver at the sight of its tentacle-fringed mouth. It might be a horrible-looking creature, but so far its purposes had not seemed inimical, and it was clearly possessed of an intelligence equal to their own.

"Are you the only one of your kind who has come?" the queen asked it.

"More await...in vessel...this emissary."

The captain of the guard stirred at this news, and the prince sent him a quelling look. It had been wise of the creatures to send a single ambassador, and Kate was further convinced the Yxleti had arrived with peaceful intentions.

"You are welcome here at the palace," Queen Victoria said. "What might we do to further relations between your kind and ours?"

"Stable rule must first be...many queens."

Queen Victoria glanced at her husband, then back to the creature.

"Do you mean our children?" Her voice was chilly.

"Not...it is Victoria Regina...reign again."

The queen's brow furrowed, and Kate understood her confusion. How could the queen reign again? She was already the monarch.

"I think, though it is simply a guess, that they mean to replicate you in some fashion," Prince Albert said in a low voice.

Kate blinked at the notion. It seemed unbelievable—but who knew what the Yxleti were capable of? After all, they journeyed between the stars. Perhaps creating a new Queen Victoria was a simple matter for them.

"Is this true?" the queen asked the Yxleti hovering a few paces before her. "You mean to re-create my very essence? It seems most ungodly."

"Each queen sleeps until reign is ended...then wakes and is self... at moment of preserve. Best... for peaceful humans always."

Queen Victoria took a step back, her mouth twisting in distaste. "I cannot countenance such a perversion."

"Then... Napoleon three will select to rule...if you decline. Humans must have single ruler."

"Bloody hell," the captain of the guard muttered. "The damnable creature's blackmailing you, your majesty."

"Of course it is." The queen's eyes narrowed. "But what choice do we have? We cannot let the French rise to ascendency."

"I have little doubt Bonaparte's nephew will leap at the chance," Prince Albert said. "Much as it might go against the laws of nature, my dear, you must accept the Yxleti's offer, or the world will end up under the thumb of a petty dictator rather than your beneficent and enlightened reign."

The queen drew in a breath through her nose, and Kate leaned forward, her chest tight. Of course her majesty would do what was best for the Empire, but what a difficult choice.

"Very well," Queen Victoria said. "We will do this thing —under three conditions."

"Tell," the Yxleti said.

"The first, that we be allowed to continue to reign as we see fit, without Yxleti intervention."

"Is already plan," the crackling voice said.

Kate regarded the creature. Of course it would make promises, but who knew if it would actually keep them?

"The second," the queen said, "is that our beloved husband also be subject to this process, so that we might have him at our side during every reign." She threaded her arm through Prince Albert's and gave him a look filled with emotion. "Will you consent to this, my dear?"

He covered her hand with his own. "I do. My place is at your side, your majesty. Year after year, to time immemorial."

The Yxleti remained motionless, but the still air was interrupted by a brief hum. After a moment, the creature turned its head toward the orb.

The crackling voice rang out. "Agreed...what is third ask."

"That you share with us the means by which you travel and explore the celestial sea. We, too, harbor the desire to set out in search of worlds unknown, and to bring the Empire to every corner of the stars. Will you aid us in doing so?"

This time there was no hesitation.

"Is intent," the Yxleti said. "In starset we come...procure duplicates of queen."

It turned and glided back to its vessel, clearly signaling that the meeting was at an end. The queen did not call after it, though her face was still filled with questions. As soon as the Yxleti entered, the oval doorway sealed shut. The now-familiar humming suffused the air, and slowly the dark orb rose.

The nearby guardsmen scrambled back, and with a whoosh of air and a steady hum, the Yxleti ascended. The orb hurtled away nearly as quickly as it had come. Kate followed its flight until it was swallowed by the searing brightness of the larger sphere.

Blinking away tears, she dropped her gaze.

"Oh my," Queen Victoria said under her breath. "What-ever have we done?"

"Either saved all of humanity, or doomed it." Prince

Albert slid his arm about the queen's shoulders. "I prefer to think the former. Steady on, my dear."

The queen nodded, then turned to the dozen people gathered on the terrace. Kate glanced about, to see that everyone wore half-stunned looks that no doubt mirrored her own. She still could not quite credit what she had just witnessed.

"Everyone," Queen Victoria said, "attend me inside. We must draw up our accounts of this momentous event. On this day, the course of the word has turned."

She swept regally toward the French doors leading into the palace. The captain of the guard followed close behind, and then the astronomers and queen's attendants.

Kate hung back a moment, casting a final look over her shoulder at the sphere that had once been nothing but a bright speck in the sky, and now was the harbinger of an unimaginable future. It cast its silvery reflection over London, offering no answers—only strangeness beyond compare.

THE LONDON UNIVERSAL TIMES, August 1907

OBITUARY NOTICE: On 10 August, Lady Kate Danville, member of the Royal Society and bestowed the title of Baroness of Canticus by Victoria I, passed quietly in her sleep. She is survived by her younger brother, nieces and nephews. A long-time advisor of the prior queen, Lady Danville was one of the few still alive in this century who witnessed the glorious arrival of the Yxleti, and was part of the council which helped usher in the new age of space exploration and global prosperity. Queen Victoria II has commissioned a statue of Lady Danville to be placed in the First Greeting sculpture garden on the landing site at Buckingham Palace.

Per Lady Danville's request, her ashes will be scattered between the stars, to float forever at peace beneath the eternal suns of the British Empire.

THE SPIDER'S SALON

The smell of baking bread filled the early-morning air along the Rue des Oranges. Marie-Solange gripped the willow handle of her shopping basket and hurried over the cobblestones, her worn boot heels tapping out a quick rhythm. She must purchase fresh baguettes and the mistress's favorite tarts, and she dared not be late. The noble family she served was punctual in their breakfast hours. Tardiness was not tolerated.

Especially not from a mulatto maid who spoke with a rustic Tahitian accent. If she lost this position, she would not be able to procure another. Not without sterling references.

As she waited in line at the patisserie, she eavesdropped on the conversations around her. The latest fashions were a topic of much discussion, especially the new hats with clock-work birds that clacked their beaks and flapped their mechanical wings. They were quite *a la mode*, although Marie-Solange found them faintly ridiculous. Beneath the gossip, however, she caught hushed speculations about France's continuing role in the clash of Empires.

"Madame Toujours is going to convince the king to attack England," one sharp-faced matron said.

"No, no," her companion replied. "She wants what is best for France—which is to close our borders entirely."

"Whatever happens," a third woman said, her expression knowing, "you can be sure that the Spider's Salon will be at the heart of it."

"Next!" the counterman cried, and Marie-Solange stepped up to make her purchases.

Her bakery items neatly secured in her basket, she sped back through the twisty Paris streets, taking as many shortcuts as possible. At one blind corner, she was nearly flattened by a steam-powered omnibus. The blare of the horn made her leap out of the way just in time, to take shelter against a nearby wall.

Heart pounding, she leaned her back against the cool stone façade. Perhaps it was foolish of her to try and save what little money she could. Perhaps she should simply accept her fate, give in to the persistent advances of the butler, and stop turning her face to the sky, hoping for more.

She drew her arm across her perspiring forehead. No. She had not come all the way to Paris simply to become another banal tale of the maid marrying the butler and working herself into an early grave. Marie-Solange straightened her back, tightened her grip on the basket, and prepared to continue on.

Then she saw it.

At first glance, it appeared to be an unremarkable black beetle clinging to the stone side of the building. But there was something strange about the shape of its body, the way its carapace caught the light.

Slowly, she bent closer to inspect the beetle. Her indrawn breath of surprise was enough to startle it, and with a quick whirr of wings it flew away, sparkling in the morning sunlight.

Had she imagined the delicate clockwork machinery making up the insect's body, the pivoting lenses of its eyes? She did not think so. But what could it mean?

The sound of a bell ringing over the Second Quarter recalled her to her duties. She pulled out her nickel-plated pocket watch, fingers absently smoothing the old, familiar dents in the casing. There was just enough time to make it back to the townhouse. Barely.

When she burst into the kitchen, the chef scowled.

"You are late," he said. "If breakfast is not served on time, it is your fault."

"I'll help." She set the basket on the weathered wooden counter.

The chef snatched a baguette and begin to slice it with precise, even strokes. "Prepare the chocolate server," he said, without looking up.

Marie-Solange carefully removed the copper-plated pot of hot chocolate from where it simmered upon the stove, and poured the liquid into the waiting vessel. While the chef arranged the bread, tarts, some brie, and sliced apples on a tray, she cranked the chocolate pot's mechanism. The ornate design of suns and stars decorating the outside began to spin, gradually whirling faster and faster. In addition to providing a pleasing display, the clockwork also contrived to keep the chocolate warm.

When she had first arrived from the islands, Marie-Solange had been astonished by such things. In Papeete, only the governor and the very wealthiest families had modern mechanicals. Now, she was more used to them. In Paris, it seemed only the very poor were without devices of some kind.

Which included herself—not that she was interested in owning such impractical things as ridiculous hats or the strange clockwork beetle she had seen. But she did not intend to be poor forever.

After serving breakfast, she had a moment to herself. She resisted the urge to slip up to her attic room and count her small but growing store of coins. If anyone saw the money, they would be suspicious.

It was not her fault the other maids had no imagination, no ambition. They preferred taking the omnibus to running about the streets on foot. They did not bother bargaining with the fish monger, who was fond of pretty girls of any color and would take a kiss in exchange for a discount. And if she kept some of the profit, what of it? Her employers received everything they had paid for.

Marie-Solange had learned from an early age to trim any margin she could off each transaction and pocket the difference. Practicing such economies, learning to charm and shrewdly negotiate in equal measure, had enabled her to save up enough for her passage to France.

And here she was. But the life she'd hoped for was still so very far out of reach.

She let out a sigh and went to stand in the kitchen gardens. The onions grew in alert green rows, and the fluffy tops of the carrots still held a trace of morning moisture. Bells rang across the city, and the puff and screech of steam-powered vehicles drifted over the weathered brick walls.

"Marie-Solange!" It was the chef, recalling her to her duties.

She gave the pale blue sky—so different from the lush azure of her home—a wistful glance, and went inside.

An hour later, Marie-Solange stepped forth again, burdened with her market basket and a long list of what the chef needed to prepare dinner. As she closed the door to the servant's entrance, a bright spot of color caught her eye.

There, clinging to the door jamb, was another beetle.

Its carapace was sheened an iridescent scarlet, bright as a fresh drop of blood. Holding her breath, she leaned forward. As she'd suspected, the body of the insect was made up of miniature gears. One lensed eye swiveled abruptly, as if surveying her. Then, with a whirr, the beetle took flight.

Unlike her earlier encounter, this bug did not disappear, a mote beneath the clouds. Instead, the beetle flew a short distance away, then alighted on the black metal side of a lamp post.

Marie-Solange went toward it.

When she came near, it launched itself into the air, this time traveling down the street. Just as she was about to lose sight of it, the insect landed on the green awning outside the book seller's.

Again, she followed. After all, it was traveling the same direction she'd intended to go. Mostly. There was no harm in seeing where it led—at least until their paths diverged.

And yet, when the scarlet beetle turned away from the market, she continued to trail it. *Just a little further*, she told herself. Who had ever seen such a wonder! Such adventures did not come every day.

She could always pay the omnibus fare, just this once, and make up any time she'd lost.

The bustle of the city surrounded her as she followed the mechanical insect; nannies pushing their charges in elaborate buggies, a street musician playing the accordion while a small mechanical ballerina danced before him, and more of those silly hats everywhere she looked.

Soon, they were in an area of Paris unfamiliar to Marie-Solange. The hiss of steam and the smell of machine oil overlay the scent of frying onions. Nervously, she read the street names as she went past, trying to orient herself. Ahead, the scarlet beetle flew, landed, waited, and flew on, seeming to beckon her to follow.

When it turned down a small alleyway, she hesitated. Behind her lay the safety of the busy street, the omnibuses that could take her back to the Second Quarter. If she stepped into this narrow, shadowed way, she might be stepping into quite a bit of trouble.

The beetle, as if sensing her trepidation, flew back toward her. It whizzed about her head in what she imagined was an encouraging manner. After a moment, it was joined by a second insect, this one turquoise-hued. They performed a brief, bejeweled dance in the air, then slowly turned and flew a short distance down the alley.

Very well. She had not come this far in life to be turned back by fear. Taking a firm grip on her basket's woven handle, Marie-Solange marched into the alley.

Twists, turns, a drift of sickly-sweet smoke, a woman's laughter falling like dust. The bright beetles flitted to a door and disappeared into a crack above it. A green door, with a delicate silver web painted upon it, and a name: *Le Salon de l'Araignée*. The Spider's Salon.

Marie-Solange halted, tongue dry within her mouth. The web upon the door was a grim warning. She had heard of this place—everyone in Paris had. It was frequented by scholars of ancient languages and brash young dandies. By women of questionable virtue and high-ranking *Assemblée* members. By free thinkers and radicals and musicians and poets.

According to some, the salon had been at the heart of at least two revolutions and a coup. It was said that the brightest inventors of the era exchanged ideas there. Marie-Solange tipped her head, gaze going to where her colorful guides had disappeared.

Before she could make up her mind whether to run away or not, the door flew open. A tall, gaunt man stood there, peering down his nose at her.

"Come in," he said, gesturing for her to enter. "Madame Toujours wishes to see you."

Madame Toujours. A shiver coursed down Marie-Solange's spine. Everyone in Paris knew that name. The spider in the heart of the web.

It was a request she doubted she could refuse. Yet she resolved to ignore the sharp point of fear corkscrewing into her belly, and proceed boldly. Sometimes, pretense was everything.

Lifting her drab skirts, she stepped over the threshold and found herself in a dimly-lit anteroom. A very large man —not the one who had opened the door—sat somnolently on a stool, his eyelids half open, taking no interest in her presence. Had she come in uninvited, she suspected he would turn into a fearsome ogre of a man.

Behind her, the door closed by itself with a thud. Another screw of fear went through her at the sound. She hoped she would be able to leave again

The thin man waited just ahead, beside a wooden panel carved with a motif of spiders. He gave Marie-Solange a sharp nod as she entered.

"Good," he said. "I am Michel, the steward of the salon."

"My name is Marie—" she began.

He waved one hand. "Do not speak. Your introductions can wait for Madame. Follow."

Splaying his hand, he placed it upon the panel. His fingers moved in a quick pattern she could not catch, and the door to the Spider's Salon swung open.

Marie-Solange blinked in surprise at what was revealed. Instead of a dark and cavernous lair, the salon was open and airy, filled with light and raucous conversation, laughter, the smell of clove-spiced tobacco, a whiff of absinthe.

People clustered around tables, playing whist and dice, or chess, or scribbling in notebooks. Beside the unlit fireplace, several black-robed scholars were engaged in debate, and in a corner two women kissed passionately.

Trying not to gawk, Marie-Solange followed the steward, and discovered that the salon was a series of interconnected rooms. She held her breath as they passed through a quiet, clandestine parlor where the guests fell silent as she went by. The next room held a pianoforte. Several couples danced a mazurka while the onlookers exhorted them to greater effort.

Every room was lit by fanciful gasoliers in the shapes of

lilies or butterflies or stars. The stained glass shapes threw light over courtesans and poets, and a dignified fellow whom she recognized from afar as a minister of the government.

It seemed as though they were winding in a spiral, each room a bit smaller than the last, and Marie-Solange made herself pay attention. If necessary, she must be able to find her way out of this web. First came the room with the butterfly lamp, and then the quiet one, then the dancing room, followed by the bar—unmistakable. She sensed they were getting closer to their destination.

The steward moved quickly and efficiently, navigating about tables and slipping around knots of patrons. Not once did he look back to make sure she was following. A few people glanced up as they passed, and she wondered what they thought to see a half-caste maid carrying an empty market basket through the rooms of the salon.

At last the steward led her to a room filled with golden light, and halted. Marie-Solange skipped back a step in order to avoid treading on his heels.

It was, indeed, the smallest of the rooms so far, and it appeared to be the last. It had space for only two carved bronze tables and a scattering of velvet-upholstered chairs. The polished parquet floor was covered by a thick Turkish carpet in shades of plum and ivory. Shelves lined the side walls, filled with books and scrolls, and a collection of mechanical birds whose glass eyes glinted in the light of the sun-shaped gasolier overhead.

Against the far wall stood a raised dais holding a gilded armchair, flanked by a silver contraption of some kind. It was not, of course, an ordinary armchair, but a throne; Marie-Solange was wise enough to see that at once. And upon that throne sat a woman, her form partially obscured by a gentleman in a long beige coat, who bowed over her hand.

"Thank you, monseigneur," the woman said. She sounded neither young nor old, neither pleased nor angry. "I am certain our association will be most beneficial."

The man nodded, then pivoted and swiftly walked from the room, mouth set, eyes full of danger. Marie-Solange resolved to immediately forget his face.

"Madame," the steward said once the gentleman was gone. "Here is the girl you requested."

"Thank you. You may leave us, Michel. Make sure we are undisturbed."

"Are you certain, Madame?"

"Quite."

With a crisp nod, Michel turned on his heel and departed. Marie-Solange stood where he had left her, clutching her basket and unsure of whether to bow, or approach Madame Toujours, or say anything at all.

Slowly, as if her bones pained her, Madame Toujours rose. She wore a scarlet dressing gown edged with burgundy velvet, and her jet black hair was caught up in combs and decorated with jeweled sticks. Even standing upon her dais she was small, smaller than Marie-Solange, but the air of authority she carried made her seem much taller.

Despite her smooth skin, age rested in the slight sag of her jowls, the lines bracketing her mouth, and especially in her piercing, dark gaze.

But the most surprising thing about her was that the famed Madame Toujours was obviously an Oriental. Her folded eyes and sallow skin could not be mistaken.

As if reading Marie-Solange's thoughts, Madame's thin lips curved into a smile.

"I am not what you expected—but then, the mistress of this salon should defy all expectation, don't you think? Tell me your name."

"I... am called Marie-Solange Travere."

One of Madame's thin eyebrows rose. "Your full name, if you please. The one you were born with."

Marie-Solange set down her woefully empty market basket so that she might fold her arms in defiance, though her heart fluttered like a frightened pigeon. "Why am I here?"

Madame Toujours regarded her a long moment, only the slight twitch of her lips betraying her thoughts. What those thoughts might be, Marie-Solange could not say. She hoped the spark in her host's dark eyes was amusement and not annoyance.

"You are here to take tea with me," Madame Toujours finally said. "Come, sit."

She motioned to one of the chairs facing her, then settled herself upon her throne.

Abandoning her basket on the plush carpet, Marie-Solange approached the dais.

"Is this because of the beetles?" she asked, perching on the velvet-upholstered seat Madame had indicated.

Madame Toujours leaned back in her chair and pulled a soft blue lap robe over her knees before answering.

"You are a very observant young woman," she said. "Every day, hundreds of mechanical bugs whir about the streets of Paris. Yet very rarely does anyone notice they are no normal insects."

Marie-Solange's fear returned in a cold wave. "Then I am here because you wish to dispose of me."

"Ha!" Madame's laughter rang out. "Good. You have a suspicious mind. But no. After we speak, if you wish it, you may return unharmed to your life as a maid."

Her breath trembling in her lungs, Marie-Solange slid to the edge of her cushioned chair. "What are you saying? Have I another choice?"

"My dear girl, there is always another choice. You know that as well as I. To stay in the islands or come to France. To sell your body, or forge credentials. To use the omnibus fare given you, or to dash over the cobblestones, counting your growing store of coins in a midnight attic."

Ice doused Marie-Solange once more. Fear, hope, fear—she was growing dizzy from the waves of emotion buffeting her. Almost, she asked what Madame meant. But there was no point in lying. It was whispered that Madame Toujours was omnipotent, and now Marie-Solange knew why.

"The beetles," she said in a low voice. "They are your spies."

Madame Toujours reached forward and pushed a button on the elaborate silver contraption beside her chair.

"Tea," she said, then leaned back. "No—they are not spies, for my mechanicals have no independent function. They simply gather information, which is brought back here to be parsed and decoded. The people who do that work and then act on the information, *they* are my spies."

"Why are you telling me this?" It was an enormous, frightening piece of knowledge, and Marie-Solange did not know why she should be singled out to receive it. Or what the consequences might be.

Faint hope sparked within her, but she quickly squelched it. *Surely not.*

"I see that you suspect." Madame nodded, then turned her attention to the tea maker, which was dispensing a stream of pale jade liquid into a bright red cup with no handle.

When she handed the cup across, Marie-Solange could see the veins in Madame's wrist beneath her paper-thin skin.

"Thank you," Marie-Solange said, her mind now racing.

If what she thought was true—foolishly vain conjecture though it might be—then she must surrender to the possibility. She must give trust for trust. If she were wrong, then at least she could take comfort in the fact that she'd taken tea with the infamous Madame Toujours. Unless, of course, the tea was poisoned.

The scent of jasmine wafted from the cup, warm and soothing. She held it up to her mouth and blew on the surface to cool it, then took a small sip.

"My name," she said, "is Marie-Solange d'Amour Teremoemoe."

Madame gave her a thin, sharp smile. "You see. It always comes down to choice." She leaned back, fingers wrapped around her own cup, and studied Marie-Solange. "Hm. You are a bastard daughter of some French soldier, but your mother's line claims royal blood. Excellent."

It was true. Her mother's people did not spend their lives running errands and delivering pastries. Marie-Solange kept her breathing even, trying to show no reaction to Madame's keen insight.

"I am old." Madame Toujours let out a small sigh. "For too long I have waited for a worthy successor. You, Mademoiselle Teremoemoe might be the one. Ah, you hide your surprise well—and I see you have already guessed at my purpose. Let me answer the doubts in your eyes. While I am old, I am not yet dying. You will have the time you need to learn the secrets every Madame Toujours needs."

"There have been others?" The instant the question left her lips, Marie-Solange knew it was foolish.

Of course there had been others. Madame Toujours, despite the name, was not immortal. It was a title, a station that passed from woman to woman.

"Always a Madame?" she asked. "Has there ever been a Monsieur Toujours?"

Approval flitted over Madame's face. Marie-Solange knew that she had allowed the emotion to be seen, for there was no doubt that Madame Toujours was a consummate actress.

"Rarely," Madame Toujours said. "And only when it is unexpected. It is our role to be different. To be remarkable. Do you think you can rise to it?"

Elation rose through Marie-Solange, accompanied by the sweet flame of vindication.

The scraping poverty she had endured in Papeete, the soul-crushing sorrow of her mother's death, the horrific conditions aboard the ship bound for France, living by her wits until she'd secured a position, and then relying even more upon cunning and secrecy; everything had brought her here, honed and hungry.

"Yes," she said, her voice strong.

"Good." Madame Toujours gave a sharp nod. "Now finish your tea and collect your basket. You will find that my steward has gathered the items you needed from your shopping expedition, and he will transport you back to your place of employment."

Ah. So that was how it would have been managed, had she refused Madame's offer.

"Would you have drugged me, so that I might forget?" she asked. "How many girls have you brought here before, that said no?"

How many had said *yes* and, despite that answer, were now gone? The question was sharp under her skin, but she dared not ask it. Yet.

"None of those things concern you at the moment." Madame's tone was dry, suggesting that Marie-Solange would not like the answers. "Tonight you will give your notice, gather your possessions, and return here to begin your training."

Marie-Solange did not bother asking how she would find her way back to the salon. She suspected this was another test; no doubt one of many in the days to come.

"Very good, Madame," she said.

"One more thing," Madame Toujours said. "From now on, I am the only one that may call you by your given name. The rest of the world shall know you as Mademoiselle Maintenant. Now, go. I shall see you this evening."

Marie-Solange set her half-full teacup on the bronze table beside her chair. She stood and curtsied to Madame Toujours, letting her rising hope shine in her eyes without speaking it aloud. No doubt her new mistress knew exactly how she felt, and Madame had already made it clear she disdained stating the obvious.

From now on, Marie-Solange was to be a student of the subtle.

Her breath lighter in her lungs than it had been for years, she scooped up her basket and strode to the threshold, where the steward had reappeared. Chin high, she led him back through the spiral of rooms, seeing each one with fresh eyes.

Here was the inception of a new dance that would sweep the Empire. Before the fireplace, scholars designed a device that could scan the stars. In the corner, an illicit passion would birth the next novel to challenge the world.

At the wooden panel leading to the anteroom, she paused. It was difficult to tell, but she thought the barest hint of a smile graced the steward's lips as he released the catch for her. Learning to open it herself must be her first undertaking, no question.

A few moments later, she was standing once more in the street outside *Le Salon de l'Araignée.*

Everything was the same. Everything was different. Sunlight slanted into the alleyway, burnishing the dust motes and making the silver spider web upon the door gleam. It no longer looked frightening.

It looked like home.

THE VISIT

Mayfair, London, 1845

The hansom cab I'm riding in smells of old vomit and smoke, and I tug at my neck cloth, trying to breathe. A loose spring in the seat pokes into my thigh with every jolt of the wheels over the cobblestones, a painful jab that I nevertheless welcome. It distracts me from thoughts of what lie ahead.

My forehead is sweaty beneath my top hat, but my gloved hands are chilled. I work them into fists—shut, open, shut. Pewter clouds squat overhead, the air heavy with the threat of rain. I should have brought my umbrella instead of my walking stick, but I craved the heft of the stick in my hand.

Shoulders tight, I send a quick glance out the window. We are close. Too close.

"Stop here." I rap the silver knob of my walking stick upon the cab's roof.

The vehicle slows, the hollow clop of the horse's hooves decelerating like a failing heartbeat.

The driver calls from above, "Are you certain, sir? The address you gave is still three blocks away."

"Yes," I say, though I am certain of nothing except the churning in my gut.

As soon as the cab stops, I fling the door open and step out. The driver scowls, but when I drop two shillings into his palm he seems satisfied.

The cab clatters away over the cobbles and I turn to face Ainsley Road. The odor of rotting vegetables clings to the back of my throat, and I breathe shallowly.

Pedestrians brush past me; ladies wearing hats bedecked with flowers and macabre stuffed birds, gentlemen laughing too loudly. I receive a few odd looks, and realize I've stood too long in this one place.

I must march onward.

Sometimes, after too much drink, my father tells tales of his days fighting against Napoleon. Their regiment was outnumbered, the casualties heavy, yet they continued advancing into the enemy's musket fire, day after day walking straight toward death. Comrades fell to either side, yet he did not falter. Even with a bullet festering in his leg he bravely carried on.

One step. Another. It isn't too bad, if I don't think about my destination.

A passing gentleman blows out a cloud of cigar smoke, nearly choking me on the acrid fumes. A baby squalls in its perambulator, its screeches lacerating the air. I keep moving. My distorted reflection keeps pace in the shop windows like a doppelganger.

At the next intersection I turn right, away from the busy street. Townhouses crouch along the road here, dimming the wan light even further. A tall wrought-iron fence parallels the sidewalk, twined round with choking vines, the sharp finials smothered in sickly white blooms. The flowers stink. Their cloying perfume fills my nose like grease.

The blank windows of the houses stare at me as I pass. The noise of carriages and pedestrians fades behind me. A chill creeps down my neck and splays like an icy hand across my shoulder blades.

My boot heels rasp over the pavement, and I hear an echo following me. I whirl, my walking stick raised, but the road is empty. There should be children playing in the gardens, ladies out for a stroll.

Instead a clammy silence shrouds the neighborhood, underscored by the march of my two feet. Every fourth step, I jab my walking stick down. Keeping count shields my thoughts from the fact that I am nearly at my destination. I envision my father's medal for bravery hanging bright in its velvet-lined case.

Too soon, the blood-red brick of Number Twenty-Eight, Ainsley Road, rises on my right. Heat flashes through me, and I halt, tasting bile. Yet I must enter, and do what I have vowed to do.

The iron gate creaks stiffly open, as if cautioning me not to come in. If only I could heed its warning. One of the filmy curtains on the second story twitches. She is watching. The gate closes behind me with a clang.

Whatever happens in the next hour, I will leave this place inexorably changed. The man I am now, destroyed forever.

Although the paved walkway leading to the front door is

smooth, it feels pitted and treacherous beneath my feet. I lean on my cane as if I'm as maimed as my father. Like him, I keep moving forward. Halfway to the stoop it begins to rain. Fat, warm drops splat down, staining the pavement and making the shrubbery hiss and rustle.

Driven by the elements, I hasten my steps. A rivulet of water gathers on my hat brim, worms down the side of my neck. The front door looms, black and shiny. A lion-headed brass knocker stares at me from the middle.

As I grip the knocker, I see it's not a lion after all, but a gorgon's head, snakes writhing about her blank eyes. I quickly release it. The thud of the knocker falling resonates through me.

Turn around, run! a treacherous voice inside me urges. Before I can act, the door opens like a black mouth gaping wide, and it's too late.

"Mr. Saintsbury, do come in." The ancient butler's voice is thin and pale, like the rest of him.

I can see the bones under the blue-veined skin of his hands as he takes my hat and gloves. Reluctantly, I hand over the walking stick. Now I'm armed only with my waning courage and the contents of the silken bag in my coat pocket. I pray it will suffice.

"Please wait in the parlor," the butler says, shuffling forward to lead me to the appointed room. "I'll notify Miss Danforth of your arrival."

I nod, incapable of saying anything. My tongue seems to have swelled to twice its normal size, leaving no room in my mouth for words. I fear that anything I say will come out in the garbled speech of a madman.

The parlor is chilly, decorated in a pale blue palette that

makes it feel even colder. I puff out a breath, expecting it to hang like a mist in the air, but it remains invisible. Tension curls through me. I pace, trudging between the empty hearth smudged with ashes and the settee upholstered in some slick fabric.

She will be here at any moment, and again the cowardly part of me wants nothing more than to flee, but I cannot. I have come this far already. I must see this through to the finish—whatever dreadful end it might bring.

I hear her light footsteps in the hallway, and turn, facing the parlor door as if facing a hail of musket fire. My heart surges with panic in my chest.

Then she enters—Miss Olivia Danforth, the woman who has haunted me for three long months, without respite. I drag my gaze up from the blue carpet to look at her.

"Mr. Saintsbury," she says, her brown eyes finding mine, her rosy lips turning up in a smile. "What a pleasure."

My heart thuds so loudly I can scarcely hear. The hallway behind her is full of shadows.

"Miss Danforth," I manage, before my mind freezes.

She moves forward, extending her gloved hand. Stiffly, I take her hand and bow over it. Her perfume is roses, sweet almost to the point of decay. When I straighten, I feel dizzy. Sweat springs on my forehead, and the once-cold room is now unaccountably too warm.

"Are you well?" She tilts her head with a quizzical look. "Do sit down—I'll ring for lemonade."

I can only nod, and let her guide me to the settee. My mind is scrabbling like a rat in a cage, biting at the bars. *Say something witty and agreeable!*

I swallow and force my tongue to loosen from the roof of my mouth.

"Are you having a pleasant afternoon?" I ask—the most inane of questions. I wish the blue rug would turn into a lake so that I might drown myself.

Her eyes smile at me. "It has taken a turn for the better. How lovely that you've come to pay a visit."

I can see questions hovering in the lift of her eyebrows, the slightly parted lips, but I cannot answer them. The edge of panic saws at my mind.

Why did I ever come? How could I possibly have thought this a wise course of action? My entire life is teetering on the brink of wreck and ruin.

The maid arrives with two cups of lemonade, saving me momentarily. I accept one with a nod of thanks. When I take a sip, the sugary, acrid taste stings my mouth. I cannot decide if it allays my nausea, or increases it.

Enough. This must end.

I set the cup down on the glossy surface of the side table and stare a moment at Miss Danforth's good-natured features—the only steady point in a room that has gone fuzzy around the edges. My heart crashes against my chest.

"Miss Danforth..." I clear my throat, swallowing back the clots of gravel lodged there.

For an instant, I'm convinced I've forgotten the silken bag. With a slash of terror, I pat at my coat pocket, then breathe again when I feel the small lump beneath my fingers.

"Yes?" She leans forward, setting her delicate hand on my forearm, and gives me an encouraging smile.

I stare at her gloved hand a moment. It is so small and fine, like an expensive porcelain cup. I am sure to break it.

"I'd best be going," I hear myself say, as if from a far distance.

Yes—that is the wisest course. Leave this house, and never return. I feel a great, ripping fire beneath my ribs. Is it relief, or crushing regret?

"So soon?" Her grip tightens. "Did you want to... ask me something?"

My neck cloth is choking me. I stare at her, those features I can see so clearly even when I am away from her; hair the color of honey, eyes like warm chocolate.

"Please stay," she says.

Her eyes stare into mine, and I cannot, after all, rise and take my leave.

"If I were to ask you a question," I say, forcing the words out awkwardly, "I fear the answer."

One corner of her lips turns up. "What if I told you there was nothing to fear?"

This is why I am risking everything. This woman. This calm assurance.

I stand at the edge of the abyss, sharp regret waiting to lacerate me as I tumble down. Then she smiles at me, and somehow the chasm is bridged.

Gods, but I cannot step across. The fall awaits me on either side.

"Edmund," she says.

It is the first time my given name has crossed her lips, and it steadies me, pushes back the roaring in my ears.

"Miss Danforth... Olivia." The sound of her name in my mouth is a talisman of hope. "I have come to ask if you..."

I am perspiring again, a wash of heat sweeping over me.

Miss Danforth grips my arm, holding fast. The air trembles between us. I close my eyes briefly, forcing back vertigo, then open them and continue.

"To ask if you will do me the very-great-honor-ofbecomingmywife." The words come out in a rush, as if I'd truly vomited out the question.

Sick and shaky, I can barely look at her. She will say *no*, and somehow I will have to command my unshackled limbs to rise and bear me away. If I am lucky, my fogged vision will lead me straight into the path of an oncoming carriage. One quick jolt, and then the blessed dark.

The blue parlor is very still. I hear the clock on the mantel whirring between each ticking second. There is a look on her face I cannot read. Surely it is shock.

Then she breathes, and smiles, and unaccountably flings her arms about my neck.

"I thought you would never ask!" she cries.

Her body is warm and soft against mine, and the scent of roses twines about me. Then she gives me a quick kiss on the lips, and I break, shatter into bright shards like a dropped mirror.

"Is that... a yes?" I ask.

"It is, you dear, brave, foolish man." She leans back and cups my face in her hands. "Of course it is. Yes, I will marry you. I've been waiting weeks now for you to ask."

I can feel the heat of her touch beneath the gloves. Gently, I take her hands in my own and, greatly daring, peel off the gloves. Skin on skin. Chimes ringing in the distance. The parlor is full of light.

"I wasn't certain." I reach into my pocket and pull out the bag, then open it. The ring is cool and glittering in my hand.

"I tried to let you know in every way possible that your suit would be accepted, short of asking you myself."

"Olivia." I say her name again, and the floor is solid beneath my feet.

She holds out her hand and I slip the engagement ring onto her finger. It fits perfectly, diamonds and sapphires winking at me, as if we share a secret.

We do. The secret in my heart, my fierce and abiding love for Miss Danforth, now spoken aloud.

I pull in a great breath of air, and feel strangely weightless. Suddenly thirsty, I raise my cup of lemonade and take a long swallow. It is a perfect balance of sour and sweet, quenching my dry mouth. She smiles fondly at me, and I smile back, relishing the unfamiliar sensation.

"I'm so excited," she says. "We must plan a grand wedding."

"Plan the wedding," I repeat. My thoughts once more march grimly forth toward the unseen enemy. Lead edges my bones. "Of course. We must plan a grand wedding."

POCKET FULL OF ASHES

The first time flames shot from Kit's fingertips, she set a gentleman's waistcoat on fire. She pulled her hand back, blinking hard. Blast! She'd missed her mark. The nob had a right fat purse too, one just ripe for snatching. But now all his attention was on himself, and the fire consuming the silk kerchief tucked in his waistcoat.

For true, Kit didn't quite believe what had happened. The fellow'd had a lucifer in his pocket that went off, surely. The bright sizzle at the end of her fingers, that was lightheadedness from not eating for nigh on two days.

She backed away quick into the market-day crowd, wrinkling her nose against the smell of scorched wool. Overhead the London sky was sullen with soot from the nearby manufactories. Lay low had always been her motto. An obvious pickpocket was asking to have her fingers lopped off—or worse.

The pedestrians on High Street milled about, half curious, half startled. Somebody called for a doctor, though by that time the fire had been extinguished by dint of the gentleman beating himself about the belly. It had only been a few flames.

Maybe he'd a still-smoldering pipe tucked away. That sudden twist of flame was none of Kit's doing.

Thanks to the hubbub, she nicked a lady's reticule and another man's pocket watch before slipping into the alleyway. She removed herself a good ways toward the Dials before stopping to lean against the damp brick wall and empty the reticule of coins.

There was a small ivory comb inside as well, inlaid with pearl. Two of the teeth were broken, so t'wouldn't be worth tuppence. She hesitated, then slipped it into the secret pocket sewed on the inside of her shirt. The coins and pocket watch went into the other side, the one reserved for Old Nellie's take.

Kit dropped the handbag into the slime. Pity, it was a flash piece, but Old Nellie had beaten it into all her squabs: take nothin' that reveals who you stole from.

Pocket watches with inscriptions, well, one of the lads would christen them, scraping the letters with the point of his knife until the words were obscured. Same with lockets.

But fancy-embroidered velvet and the like had to be discarded.

Her spoils taken care of, Kit lifted her hands in the dim light between the buildings and studied them. Her flesh looked normal as ever—grime embedded under her ragged nails, dirt darkening her skin so she looked like a foreigner from the Raj. Her fingers seemed the same, too. She wiggled them experimentally, pointed at the wall, and squinted. Nothing happened.

Right, then. Flames leaping from her fingertips? She gave

a shaky laugh. It was her imagination, and the last bit of fever that had kept her from the streets for three days.

Old Nellie was a firm believer in one day of broth and rest, and then back to work. If you couldn't pry yourself up from the thin pallet, well then, lie there until you could, but no gruel or kind words would come your way.

Kit had never been so sick before. She'd alternated between burning hot, then freezing. Her friends Tiller and Tuck had done what they could; lending her their blankets when she shivered uncontrollably, bringing her water. Finally, after three days, she'd been able to rise and feed herself the last scrapings of congealed porridge in the pot.

Her stomach clenched with hunger, but if she took some of the coins and bought herself a meat pie, Old Nellie would smell it on her. Better return to the roost and hope for a bite of something than court a beating that would put her back on her pallet, this time with welts and bruises on top of a fever-addled brain.

She went back by way of Tiller's haunt—a corner in Westminster where the younger beggars usually had luck looking piteous. Matrons on the way to chapel always threw a few coins, and once a baker had given Tiller three loaves of bread. Burned on the bottom, but Old Nellie's flock had gone to bed that night with full stomachs.

"Hoy," she said, sidling up to the small, one-legged figure holding out a grimy wooden bowl.

She glanced inside. A few ha'pennies lay there, catching the dull pewter light of the sky overhead.

"Kit!" Tiller's brown eyes lit. "Got yer takings for the day?"

"Aye. Was hoping for a bite. You?"

He frowned, the expression bringing out the hollows in his cheeks. "Not yet."

Kit glanced around, and didn't see any eyes or ears lurking to get them in trouble.

"Here." She fished in her pocket and pulled out one of the shillings from the stolen reticule.

Palming it, she dropped it into his hand. He didn't look—didn't need to. The heft and texture of a shilling were unmistakable, and Old Nellie had her birds learning from day one how to sort coins by feel alone.

"C'mon then," Kit said, giving Tiller a hand up.

She tossed him his crutch, too, and was mostly patient as he hobbled down the soot-darkened street. Finally, just when she was going to say something snappish, Tiller ducked into a doorway. He tugged his trouser leg up and quickly unbound his right foot, letting out a groan as he unbent his leg from where it had been tied, calf to thigh.

"My foot's all pins and needles," he said, gingerly taking a few steps.

"Good thing you've a crutch," Kit said. "Supper'll be all gone if we don't step it up."

Tiller nodded, and with the aid of the crutch they hurried toward the river. The stench of the Thames was worse than usual, and she wrinkled her nose. Still, it was best to go home along the bank, then cut over past Whitehall. Didn't need the authorities giving them the eye and turning their pockets out.

By the time they left the riverbank, Tiller was striding out freely, the crutch tucked under his arm.

"Bind t'other leg tomorrow," Kit said. "The nobs'll never notice."

"They don't want to look too close at beggars," Tiller agreed. "Some days I'm even missing a hand 'stead of a leg and it's all the same to them. Piss on the gentry."

"Hush," Kit said, not from any sympathy with the high-born, but to ward off trouble.

Too late. A burly copper stepped from the alley in front of them. He wasn't in uniform, but Kit could smell the authority rolling off him, ale and metal mixed together. She turned and made a dash for it, but Tiller was too slow.

"You, there!" The copper grabbed Tiller's arm and swung him around. "Been working the streets, have you?"

"Let him go," Kit said. She'd stopped out of reach, mind working furiously.

In the nearby alley a waste barrel overflowed with rotten vegetable peelings and soiled rags. If she threw an armful of trash at the copper, would he let go of Tiller long enough for them to get away? She sized the man up. Blast, but he was a brute. Tiller looked like a stick doll in his grasp.

But she had to do *something*. Already the policeman was going through the pockets of Tiller's patched coat, while the boy squirmed. Another few seconds and he'd find the small store of coins, and either pocket them himself or take Tiller in. Old Nellie would be steaming mad, whichever way it went. And that always meant beatings and short rations for everyone.

"Get off!" Tiller jabbed at the copper, but his blows had as much effect as a fly buzzing at a horse.

The crazy image of flames danced across Kit's vision, and she shook her head. Surely not.

But just maybe...

She whirled and splayed her fingers wide, pointing them

at the rubbish barrel. Nothing happened, except the copper gave her a quizzical look, and she felt like a bloody fool.

Right then. When left with nothing else, resort to fakery.

"Fire!" she yelled. "Down the alley, there."

Hopefully it would distract Tiller's captor, and the both of them could scarper.

"Where?" The man hauled Tiller closer to where she stood, and Kit backed warily away.

"There!" She pointed again at the imaginary flames, then blinked as a stream of fire careened from her fingertips.

With a loud *whump*, the barrel went up in flames. For a half second, they all stared at the blaze, then Kit grabbed Tiller's elbow, wrenched him free, and the two of them pelted down the uneven cobblestones.

"Hey!" The copper looked at them, then back at the burning bin. But only an idiot would leave a fire unchecked to pursue two ragged street urchins.

She and Tiller skidded around the corner, then kept going, neither of them speaking until they'd gone deep into the Dials and were approaching the roost.

"Not a word," Kit said.

Tiller turned to her, his eyes round, and she could see a bit of fear seeping in as he looked at her.

"Stop it." She gave him a punch to the shoulder. "Tisn't anything. A trick. Now keep yer maw shut."

Despite her words, she knew deep down in her bones that this newfound power, whatever it was, amounted to more than just trickery. And she knew, just as sure, that if Old Nellie found out, a mort of trouble would follow.

Kit glanced down at her unremarkable hands.

Danger was perching on her shoulder like a black crow,

she reckoned, and she didn't know how to shoo it away. Pray God and all the little angels it didn't get so hungry it pecked her eyes out.

OLD NELLIE LET her keep the comb, after pointedly asking whether Kit had broken the teeth off herself. She truthfully said no, and Old Nellie grunted her consent.

But Kit's flash of satisfaction faded when Old Nellie stooped closer and took her chin in a hard, implacable grip.

"Reckon there's a pretty enough face there," she said, "under all that dirt. You bleed yet?"

"No'm," Kit said, her breath rising in her lungs.

"Hmph." Old Nellie's creased face was too close, her eyes boring into Kit's. "Tell me when you do."

Kit nodded, and shut her eyes in thanks as soon as the older woman turned away.

But Kit was fourteen, or roundabouts. Small for her age, but her body was changing. She'd started binding old rags about her chest and belly, to conceal the new swell of her bosoms. On the street she was still taken for a boy, but how long would that last?

As soon as she started to curve out a bit more, it was farewell to the roost and into the life of a scarlet woman. A life Kit most sincerely did not want. She'd seen the cares and troubles hammer down on the girls, until a year looked like ten upon their worn faces and bodies.

Old Nellie held no truck with the selling of children, but once a girl got her shape, even if she was missing half her teeth, off to the red district she went. One less mouth to feed, according to Old Nellie. Kit had seen her counting coins after Tansy had gone. There was no stopping that fate.

Unless she up and ran.

She'd have to go far though. Out of London entirely. The thought made her shiver. What would she do in the country-side? Cows had no pockets for picking, and every villager knew one another. A thief in their midst would be clear as a clot of mud on a lady's white gown.

She could leave England, but on the streets she'd heard whispers of trouble brewing. Armies mustering in Spain and Turkey and even the reclusive island monarchy of Carventia, where it was said that even the women were fierce fighters and babies were given knives before they could walk.

After a supper of crusts and thin soup, Kit lay awake for a long while, listening to the other children snore and snuffle in their sleep. Once a rat nosed out of the wall. Kit lifted one finger and concentrated, trying to find the place inside her where the fire dwelt. It felt like pepper in the back of her nose, and a twitch of frustrated anger.

A trail of sparks flew from her fingertip, singing the rodent's fur. With an affronted squeak, it skittered back into its hole.

Kit smiled and folded her hands over her chest like they were made of gold and rubies. This strange new power changed everything.

For once, she had the hope of making a better life for herself. Even if it meant she had to burn half the Dials down on the way out.

A LARGE CROWD milled at the dockside, eagerly awaiting the arrival of the Carventian ambassador to England. The smell of dead fish buried in mud wafted in gusts from the Thames, but Kit didn't care about that, nor the curved prow of the armored vessel being escorted upriver by royal ships of the navy.

It made for a good distraction though, making it plumb easy to slip bits of fine out of pockets while the nobs craned their necks to watch the ships' progress.

"Divide up, like at market," Old Nellie had instructed them, her eyes gleaming. "It'll be a fat crowd, easy pickings. Don't get too near the queen and her guard. Ah, we'll eat well, and a day off tomorrow for the lot of you, provided you do yer jobs."

"And we don't get caught," Tuck muttered.

He'd been in a black mood the past month, ever since his growth came on. It was harder to dodge and dart about a throng once you were full-sized, and Tuck was getting near the mark. Kit figured this might be the last time Old Nellie sent him out with the rest of the flock before turning him over to a new master. Fighter, maybe, or something rougher. Tuck knew it, too.

Kit had given him a sympathetic jab in the ribs, but he'd only frowned back at her.

He was working the back of the crowd now, near enough the dockside alleyways he could duck out if he were caught catching some gentleman's coins from a slit pocket.

Keeping a genial smile upon her face, Kit moved easily, letting the throng of people carry her forward, slipping a bit to one side, then the other. There was a particular lady in a green velvet dress who seemed quite careless of her matching reticule. A quick jostle and snip, and the purse would be Kit's.

A petite girl in a dark blue skirt and patched coat nabbed the reticule first, tucked it under her coat, then had the cheek to nod and curtsey to the oblivious lady before moving away. Kit caught the girl's eye then had to smother a laugh. Tiller had found a black wig from somewhere, and was just pretty enough to pass for a girl. He winked at her, then disappeared back into the crowd.

"The ship's almost here!" a man called.

The crowd responded like a single creature, surging forward to the river's edge. Kit was caught up in the push, and found herself nearly shoved off the dock, the thick waters swirling just below the toes of her scuffed boots. She scrambled back, but not far enough to lose her new vantage point.

The Carventian ship was furling its scarlet sails, and now was under steam, with one royal frigate ahead, and one behind. White puffs drifted from the smokestacks at the back of the foreign vessel. At the prow stood a resplendent figure in bright yellow robes. Kit couldn't tell if it was a lady, or a gentleman all got up in strange garb. Around her, the crowd buzzed with speculation.

"They say the Grand Viceroy wants to marry the queen."

"She's already got a husband, what!"

"More's the merrier...." Coarse laughter followed that statement.

"I don't trust 'em. Centuries the Carventians hole up, firing on our ships, forbidding civilized contact... They're up to no good, mark my words."

A blaze of red distracted Kit, and she realized she'd

fetched up a mite too close to where Queen Victoria herself stood, her honor guard of lobster-backs attending her. At the queen's side hovered her husband, Prince Consort Albert, watching the ship approach with a grim eye. Mayhap the rumors were true.

The queen looked calm and dignified, her glossy brown hair braided back, her thin nose regally lifted. Kit regarded her for a moment. What would it be like, to be a queen?

As if feeling her stare, Queen Victoria's head turned slightly, and her eyes met Kit's. Blimey! There was strength in that gaze and a touch of worry, but no revulsion as she held Kit's stare.

Belatedly, Kit dropped her gaze to the cobbles, then scuttled away, heart racing. The queen had actually looked at her as if she were a real human being, not a piece of street trash.

Boom!

Kit jumped, then realized the sound was the bass drum of a marching band. Three more thuds, and the air was filled with the blare of trumpets and reeds, playing a musical welcome. The Carventian ship was close enough now that Kit could see the figure at the prow smiling. Despite the long, gaudy robes, she decided it was a man from the jut of his chin.

Slowly, the vessel pulled up to the edge of the dock. The two ships of the royal navy stood by, and Kit glimpsed the dark ports on the sides, where cannons lurked. The Carventian's anchor splashed into the water, the chain rattling down to the dredged-out riverbed. Deckhands scurried to remove a section of the railing, and Kit could see a long wooden gangplank being readied. Some of the queen's guard went to clear a space for the plank to land. The band ended their march with a triumphant chord as the gangplank touched British soil.

A few of the Carventian sailors ran down to secure the walkway, then turned and waved at the ship. The crowd quieted a bit, and Kit could hear the flag of Carventia flapping in the breeze overhead. She glanced at the tallest mast, trying to make out the image. A falcon on a blue background, tearing the head off a snake. Loverly.

A thin fellow dressed in black livery stationed himself at the top of the gangplank.

"Attention!" he cried, in accented English. "The Grand Viceroy of the great nation of Carventia!"

The crowd gave a cheer, and Queen Victoria stepped forward as the yellow-robed man began to descend the plank. Behind him came a retinue of blue-robed warriors. At least they moved like soldiers, with crisp precision.

Halfway down the gangplank, with the gray Thames curling beneath, the Grand Viceroy halted.

"Carventia sends to England it's most sincere regards," he said, his voice rich and full, and barely accented at all. He raised his arms, yellow robes fluttering, then brought his hands down sharply. "And regrets."

It was all the warning they had. The viceroy turned his back on Queen Victoria, waiting at the foot of the gangplank. The blue-robed men parted around him as he returned to the ship, then they drew their swords and swarmed forward, blades glinting in the sunlight.

The queen's guard sprang forward, meeting the first onslaught with their bayonets, but more Carventian warriors were on the gangplank, and massing on the deck of the ship. Crossbow quarrels flew, and Kit watched in horror as Prince Albert, shielding the queen, took a shot to his upper arm. The guards yelled and closed ranks around the Royal couple, and on the river, the navy ships opened fire on the Carventians.

Screaming and cursing, the crowd turned to flee, becoming a mindless beast intent only on escape. Kit hung back, fear hammering through her veins. She didn't want to risk being trampled—but to stay at the dockside was sure death. The clash of swords and cries of the soldiers sent shivers through her.

She caught a glimpse of the queen's face, pale and determined as she and her guards slowly retreated from the dockside. They were hindered by the bulk of the crowd, and even as Kit watched, one of the guards fell, his red coat stained darker by his blood.

The heavy scrape of metal made her turn, to see that the Carventian ship had opened its portholes. The lethal bores of cannons emerged, pointed right directly at the queen. And the fleeing crowd. And Kit.

Ah, no.

Fires had broken out on the deck of the foreign vessel, but the sailors ignored them in favor of pressing the attack. Clearly, the peaceful envoy had all been a sham. Likely 'twasn't the Grand Viceroy at all, but some foolish fellow willing to give his life for his country.

Kit wasn't near as willing, though. Not without a fight.

She narrowed her eyes. There were powder kegs in that ship somewhere. And she had the flames to light them.

Standing firm, she splayed her fingers wide and summoned up all the fear, all the anger and injustice she dwelt with every day. White-hot flames shot from her fingertips, igniting the gangplank and the blue robes of the warriors. Kit ignored their screams as they fell into the river.

She raised her hands, and the railing sprang into fire, the furled sails smoldered then lit, the rigging and tarred deck burst into flame.

But it wasn't enough. She pointed to the front porthole, shooting a thin stream of fire from her index finger. It sizzled, burning through her nerve endings, but flew true into that square of shadow. Screams issued from the gunners and the front cannon exploded with a chest-rattling *whump*.

The second cannon fired, and Kit ducked as the cannon-ball flew above her head. Was the queen safe yet? What of her friends?

She pointed again, this time amidships, but only a flicker emerged from her fingertip. Her head ached something fierce, and her vision blurred. Her flames had been spent. Indeed, she felt nearly burned to ashes herself. Best hope the royal navy boarded the enemy ship soon and disabled that second cannon.

Kit dropped her hands to her knees and bent, trying to catch a breath past the tang of powder and smoke in the air. She glanced to the side, to see that Queen Victoria, Prince Albert, and their guards had almost reached the safety of the buildings. On the far side of the docks, more redcoats were arriving at a run. Purposeful motion caught Kit's eye; two of the guard heading her way.

"You, lad," one of them called. "Come with us."

"There's a reward for what you did," the other added, as if she were too stupid to see past the honey baiting the trap. She weren't about to trade one kind of captivity for another.

Pulse beating fast in her chest, she turned and made a wavering dash for the back end of the retreating crowd.

One of the guards sprinted after her and caught her arm in a tight grip. "Got you!"

"Let me go." Kit tried to peel his fingers off, but he held her fast. She bent, ready to bite his hand, when the sky lit with a flash of flame.

On its heels came a tremendous explosion as the Carventian ship blew itself to smithereens. Debris rained down on the crowd, and the guardsman's fingers slackened.

Quick as thought, Kit twisted free, then eeled between two portly gentlemen trying to make their way through the screaming crowd. She kept going, using her elbows and knees to clear a path until she was certain she'd lost her pursuers.

Yet the guards would keep looking for her. They'd seen the fire blazing from her fingers. And when they inevitably found her, then what?

She'd still be a bird in a cage, just with different masters. While the queen might prove a kinder mistress than Old Nellie, Kit was bone-tired of jumping when someone else yelled.

No. She was going to be captain of her own bloody life from now on.

A hand caught her arm, and she whirled, panic sticking in her throat until she recognized Tuck.

"I saw what you done," he said, looking her up and down. "You running?"

"Aye." It was the only answer.

"I'm coming with you." He said it like a simple fact, no room for argument.

Kit pinched her lips together, then nodded. Truly, if he'd seen her power, 'twas probably the simplest answer to keep him with her. His increasing brawn could prove useful, too.

"Me too," Tiller piped, pinching her other arm.

"Right then." She could hardly let Tuck come and tell Tiller no. "Give me your wig."

It would do for the beginnings of a disguise. His skirt too, if she could fit it around her middle.

"Not here, though." Tuck jerked his head toward one of the warehouses.

He was right, the crowd was thinning, the last bit of the panicked stampede now dissipating into weary swirls of motion. A few bodies lay groaning on the cobbles, and Kit saw with dismay that the fire from the immolated ship had spread onto the docks. She hoped the fire brigade was at the ready.

A few blue-robed warriors were making a stand, but the redcoats would dispatch them soon enough. The Carventians had been pure fools to think they could assassinate the queen on her home soil.

'Cept they nearly done, if hadn't been for Kit.

She looked down at her ordinary hands. Had she used up all her power with that bright and searing surge? And had it been worth it? The thump of her heart beat a weary *yes*.

"Old Nellie'll skin us alive, if she catches us," Tiller said.

"The red marines'll do worse," Tuck said. "At least, to us. Don't know about you, Kit."

"Then we'd best put some miles under our feet." She shoved her hands into the pockets of her trousers. "That purse Tiller nabbed should buy us fares all the way to Scotland."

"Too cold there, I hear." Tuck frowned. "I say we go to Italy."

Italy. Now that was a curiously intriguing thought.

"I've it all planned out," Tiller said as they ducked into the shadowy cave of the warehouse. "We're traveling magicians, right? Sleight of hand—we can thank Old Nellie for that—and tumbling tricks—that's me. And of course, the fire." He gave Kit a hopeful, wary glance.

She took a deep breath and held up one finger, rummaging about in her mind for the spark. *There.*

A tiny blue flame flickered, then went out. Relief made her feel slack as a marionette with the strings let go. Small, yes, but the fire was regathering. She could tell.

She snatched the wig from Tiller's head. It was grimy and tangled, likely infested, but it would do.

Pushing back the coarse black strands, she grinned at her companions. "Gentleman, I believe the world awaits the debut of the fabulous, fire-wielding trio known as The Amazing Karamesvkys!"

Deep inside, the embers began to glow.

The future lay ahead, filled, no doubt, with adventures and trouble in equal measure. But bright and beckoning. A spark. A flame. A burning star blazing through the dark.

LADY ELIZABETH'S BETROTHAL BALL

Her Royal Highness Elizabeth Calloway von Saxe-Roth, sole daughter of the Duke of Albany, stood before the grand double doors leading to the ballroom and tried to breathe past the tightness of her corset. The last taste of free air ought to have been sweeter in her lungs, but she was perspiring in her extravagant gown and elbow-length gloves.

Her heavy coiffure weighed upon her head, making her neck ache, and her diamond earbobs pulled uncomfortably on her ears. The nano-lifters in her skirt swayed the gossamer fabric up and down, but that was the only buoyant thing about her. Her soul was cased in lead.

Beyond those tall, gilt-encrusted doors, down the endless staircase, lay her doom.

"Don't look so nervous," her lady's maid, Tilly, had admonished as she'd helped Elizabeth dress in preparation for the ball. "'Tisn't as if you're going to your execution, milady. You'll end this night a betrothed woman!"

Yes, and that was the problem.

Elizabeth as she was would cease to exist, and some

other creature would take her place. A future wife. A prize to be won, auctioned off to the highest bidder.

She had contemplated running away, but Father would send his men after her. Even the farthest star systems lay within reach of the British Empire and its nobility. As an eligible daughter of royal blood, she would be hunted down for the rest of her life. They would never simply let her go.

That was no existence—to subsist as fugitives, fleeing from planet to planet. Not for her, and not for Odile.

"*Cherie*," Odile had said, stroking her hair as they lay together upon her narrow bed. "You have a future, a destiny, that does not include me."

"What good is being a member of the royal family, if I'm powerless?" Elizabeth had drawn a ragged breath, binding the cracks in her heart to keep it from splitting wide open. "I love you."

"And I, you." Odile had met her gaze, her green eyes clear as she spoke the truth. "But I am a foreigner, and so far beneath you it is a matter for laughter. I am a tradeswoman, a mechanic, and you, a princess."

"I don't care."

Those words had become a chant, lodged deep in Elizabeth's chest. *I don't care.*

The duke insisted she marry soon. Too much trouble could be stirred up by the fact of an unattached royal daughter. Even in London, the rebel faction was active, and any chance to harm the queen or her family would be seized upon.

"You might be kidnapped, held for ransom. Used to breed future pretenders to the throne." Her father's voice was hard and uncompromising.

"I don't care."

He'd looked as if he wanted to slap her, and she lifted her cheek in invitation. Instead, he'd turned on his foot and stalked away.

"You will be the loveliest girl there tonight," Tilly had said, affixing the heavy diamond necklace about her neck. "This ball gown turns your eyes the exact shade of periwinkles, and brings out the russet in your hair. So becoming!"

"I don't care."

"Oh, darling, being a married woman is wonderful," her mother had said, kissing the air above her cheek. "I'm so delighted. Which gentleman will you choose? Aren't you excited? It's just like a fairy tale."

"I don't care."

But of course she did, desperately.

She had tried to explain to her mother that she did not find men attractive in the least, but Lady Albany had waved her hand and declared that a few weeks in the marriage bed would certainly change her mind. And if not, there were any number of talented young men who would be happy to please the duke's daughter. For a small fee, or perhaps a trinket of favor.

The thought turned Elizabeth's stomach. She only wanted Odile's kisses, the shape of a body pressed against hers that mirrored her own.

From the other side of the double doors, a trumpet sounded a fanfare. The brassy notes rang through the air, calling attention to the head of the stairs, as they were meant to. It was Elizabeth's cue to enter.

The footmen pulled the doors open. Elizabeth lifted her chin and stepped forward. The noise and smell of the ballroom struck her like a blow: high pitched laughter, the last notes from the string quartet as they quieted, a mix of cologne and rose water and sweat that made her eyes sting.

She blinked three times. Dukes' daughters were taught at an early age to present a composed face to the world, no matter the firestorm raging inside. Or the imminent threat of annihilation.

There was one thing, however, that her parents had neglected to take into consideration.

What if no one actually offered for their daughter?

It was an enormous obstacle to overcome, of course. The prestige of her breeding alone made Elizabeth a catch even had she been hideous (which she was not), or unintelligent (a plus in some gentlemen's eyes), or clumsy, or tasteless, or any number of flaws in appearance or personality that could be overlooked due to the fact that she was the Duke of Albany's daughter.

Indeed, she found it quite unlikely that anyone actually saw *her*, Elizabeth, the young woman beneath the royal veneer, the expensive nano-mechanical gown and glittering diamonds.

She stepped to the top of the stairs and paused, one gloved hand clenched on the balustrade. Her heartbeat fluttered recklessly.

Tonight, she would make them see.

Her reputation would die a spectacular death, and her parents might well disown her, if they did not lock her up for decades. Ruin was preferable to the alternative, however.

The assembled guests turned to the grand stairwell, conversations trickling to a close as their gazes fixed on Elizabeth.

"Ladies and gentleman," yet another footman announced. "Her Royal Highness, Princess Elizabeth Calloway von Saxe-Roth of London."

The trumpet blasted a run of notes, and the crowd applauded as Elizabeth slowly began to descend the stairs.

She had considered deliberately tripping, to land sprawled and disheveled, possibly bleeding or with a broken limb. But that would only elicit pity and a postponement of the betrothal ball. It was no permanent solution.

She had also thought of flinging herself from a high balcony onto the polished marble floor, but no. For one thing, Odile would never forgive her, and for another, Elizabeth was too fond of her own life to seriously entertain the idea of taking it.

Every gaze fastened upon her. She counted the carpeted treads as she went. Two. Three.

Some faces were appreciative, some avaricious. Some contemplated advantageous futures, others had lust for power writ upon their expressions. The women looked jealous, or scornful, or pitying, depending on their natures.

Five steps down, out of fourteen stairs. Elizabeth held her head high.

It was not too late to surrender. She could continue the full flight down, reach the bottom and let the crowd close about her like dark water over her head. She could smile and say empty words, and meekly go into a bleak and soul-killing future.

"It is not so bad, darling," her mother had said when she came to deliver the diamond necklace. "Men can be wrapped about your little finger, if you only care to exert yourself a little. And the true power is behind the throne, as they say."

She let out her usual laugh, so throaty it almost sounded natural. Sometimes, though, Elizabeth could see the trapped look in her mother's eyes, hear the brittle edge to her words, each one weighed so carefully.

"I don't like gentlemen," Elizabeth had said.

"Now, now." Lady Albany had patted her hand. "When you are married, the first few times will be difficult, I daresay. But after that you may develop a taste for it."

Elizabeth had narrowed her eyes, and said nothing.

Ever since she was a girl, she'd known she had no attraction to the male gender—at least not in the fashion expected of man and wife. She did not dislike men in general. Only the thought of lying with them.

Halfway down the stairs, she stopped. Her heart was thudding in her chest, her gloves damply adhering to her palms. This was her moment. Act now—or be forever lost in the role society had set for her. Obedient wife. Mother of heirs. Pretty bauble to be displayed hanging from her husband's arm.

No.

She swallowed, her throat dry.

"Dear guests," she said, pitching her voice to carry. "Thank you for attending. However, I have a confession to make."

That riveted the drifting attention. At the foot of the stairs, she saw her father scowl. She must finish quickly, before he strode up and dragged her from the ballroom.

With a quick flick of her fingers, Elizabeth activated the specially modified nano-lifters in her gown and coiffure. The dress split open and floated away, to reveal Elizabeth wearing close-fitting black trousers, boots, and a low-cut shirt that revealed the shocking dragon tattoo winding across her chest.

The gasps of surprise were gratifying, but even better were the shrieks of dismay as her wig—made of her own hair —lifted from her shaven head. It tumbled to the floor, an inanimate, hairy pet.

"Elizabeth!" Her father, the duke, took the stairs two at a time, and caught her shoulder in a hard grasp.

"Wait," she called, stripping off her gloves and letting them fall. Her arms were inked with snakes and flowers, a mad riot of color. "I must admit the truth—I have had carnal congress, and am no longer an innocent!"

Her words rang through the ballroom. Lady Albany fainted, and was caught by two nearby gentlemen as the crowd erupted. The noise of shocked speculation rose like a rogue wave, washing over her. Later, Elizabeth would be able to savor the looks of dismay and revulsion, but for now her father had her in his grasp.

"Enough." The duke turned his back on the hubbub and hauled her up the stairs.

He towed her through the double doors and down the hall to the wing of private rooms.

"You are an idiot," he said, his voice furious, though his expression remained set. A duke never outwardly displayed his rage on his face. "How dare you ruin your reputation, and your chances of making a brilliant match? Who will have you, now, after that ridiculous display?"

"No one, I hope." Her voice shook, but triumph raced through her.

"We will salvage this yet," her father said, eyes dark with anger. "For now, you are confined to your rooms."

He thrust her into her sitting room and slammed the door. She heard the snick of the lock, and then her father giving instructions to the footmen to guard her well.

Despite the trembling in her legs, the soreness of her newly tattooed skin, Elizabeth smiled. She had won. Oh, her parents did not yet know it, but by the morrow Elizabeth's sordid tale would be broadcast by every gossip rag in the galaxy. Her Royal Highness Elizabeth's reputation would be soiled beyond repair—no matter that half of the story she had sent to the news reporters was complete fabrication. The damage would be done—never to be undone.

She went to her wardrobe and removed the length of rope, her store of coins, and the small pack holding a knife, a change of clothing, a thermal kit, and two outbound tickets to Hermetica's moon. As she closed the wardrobe door, the mirror caught the image of a small, determined young woman wearing a diamond necklace—incongruously bright above the indigo dragon inked into her skin.

The necklace, sadly, must remain in London. As would the tattered remains of Princess Elizabeth Calloway von Saxe-Roth's reputation.

She tied the rope around the bedpost of her heavy bed, then opened the near window to the night. It was warm for May, the scent of earth and green things borne on the breeze. Elizabeth glanced once more about her bedroom—her prison—the ashes of her past.

Then, rope coarse against her palms, she climbed over the sill. Regret crouched on her left shoulder, fear on her right, like sentinel gargoyles. What had she done? The enormity of her actions nearly bore her crashing to the dew-speckled ground.

Would she forever grieve this night?

What if Odile refused to come with her?

Perhaps all that awaited her was an ignominious pauper's death on some distant mining asteroid, her passing unknown and unmourned.

She leaned back, booted feet finding purchase on the brick wall as she let herself down. The touch of earth beneath her feet steadied her, eased the sharp breaths binding her lungs.

The indigo dragon and her own desperation would bear her forward, into her new life. The princess was gone—left behind with jewels and gowns and golden coins. In her place stood itinerant Liza Roth.

A girl with no title. No family. No fortune.

Only a future that was entirely her own.

THE WORTH OF RUBIES

London, 1848

I t was an astonishingly warm night, for May. Isabelle Strathmore sat on the velvet-upholstered chair beside her mother and plied her fan, trying not to breathe too deeply of the perfume-rank air in Lady Frampton's salon. At least the windows were open, letting in the occasional waft of breeze.

The heat and closeness of the room did not seem to trouble her brother, Richard, the star performer of the evening's musicale. He played the piano confidently, the bittersweet strains of Chopin's *Farewell Waltz* curling around the two-dozen or so listeners. The ones who were awake, at any rate.

A pity so many of the gentry could not appreciate good music. The gaslight sconces had been extinguished, leaving only a candelabra beside the piano. The dimness, combined with the warmth, had proved too much for some of the gathering's less-enthusiastic listeners. Isabelle had counted three distinct snores within ten minutes of the program's commencement.

Richard would play Beethoven next, and roust the sleepers. She smiled at the thought.

Another bit of breeze managed to slip in through the Palladian windows, and Isabelle took a deep breath. There was a heavy coolness now in the wind, mixed with the usual taste of London soot, something that hinted of ferocious rain. Perhaps the unseasonable heat was about to break.

Beethoven *and* a thunderstorm—wouldn't that be lovely?

The candles flickered, the light gleaming over her brother's fair hair. He seemed oblivious, his fingers striding along the keys. Then another flurry of wind came, lifting the pages of music and swirling them to the floor like refugee birds. Richard paid them no mind—he played on, the notes secure in his memory.

One of the nearby snorers awoke with a snort. Servants moved quietly to the windows, ready to close them if a storm descended.

Richard played the final run of notes, descending to a mournful chord. As if on cue, a sudden gust of wind stormed through the open windows. The candles blew out at once, cloaking the room in twilight. There was a smattering of bemused applause, broken by a babble of voices. Around Isabelle, several people had taken to their feet in alarm. Her mother set one hand on her arm.

"One moment," a voice called—their hostess, Lady Frampton. "Please, remain calm. We shall have light in a moment."

There was a scurry of barely-seen movement as the

footmen scrambled to comply, then the flare and tang of phosphor as the first sconce was lit. Isabelle blinked at the brightness. The crowd was beginning to settle, when a piercing cry cut the air.

"My necklace!" A large woman in a red gown stood, hands at her neck, her expression wild. "Someone has stolen my rubies!"

An immediate hubbub broke out. Lady Frampton's calls for calm went unheeded. The shrill queries of the other ladies overlaid masculine tones of gruff consternation. From the corner of her eye, Isabelle caught movement—a tall figure slipping out into the hallway. Had there been someone standing there, beside the door?

Yes, she recalled him now—a frowning, black-haired man who had put her in mind of one of the most disagreeable fellows of her acquaintance. His abrupt departure was beyond suspicious, but she had no idea who he was. When she rose in an attempt to follow, her mother took her elbow.

"Stay close, Isabelle," Lady Strathmore said.

"But—"

"The musicale is over. Come, Richard looks a bit bewildered. You may explain to him why stolen rubies take precedence over Beethoven."

Isabelle sighed and cast a glance over her shoulder. The empty hallway held no answers.

THE NEXT MORNING, sunshine streamed through the east-facing windows of the breakfast room, making the yellow-striped wallpaper almost too bright to bear. Isabelle squinted, her mind still fuzzy with sleep, and let out an invisible sigh. London was too hot, and she longed to return to their country estate. Which they would—as soon as Papa had finished his presentations for the Royal Botanical Society. She slipped into her seat and accepted a cup of tea from her mother.

"It would appear Richard's performance last night was an eventful one," Papa said, shaking his copy of the Times. "It has even displaced the headlines decrying the opening of Queen's College for Women. I'm sorry I missed the spectacle. Stolen rubies? Who knew that such dreadful and base criminals were lurking among the upper gentry?"

Isabelle added a lump of sugar to her tea. The silver sugar-tongs clacked loudly when she set them back down.

"Do the police have any suspects?" Isabelle's mother inquired, calmly buttering her toast.

"Not a one. They are hard at work, of course."

"Of course," Richard said, around a mouthful of eggs. "I wish I could have at least finished the performance."

"Do not speak with a full mouth, dear," their mother said. "I'm afraid a crime overshadows a musicale in every case."

"People have no sense of priority." Papa set the newspaper beside his now-empty plate. "I'm certain my lecture at Kew Gardens today will be sadly eclipsed by gossip and speculation. If not about the theft, then about the college. No-one wants to hear of hybrid orchids."

"Pensley will," his wife said. "You know he's been following your work. We will all go, at any rate."

"Must we?" Isabelle asked, while Richard let out a groan.

"Yes. We shall depart promptly at two-o-clock."

THE LECTURE HALL at Kew Gardens was filled, the soaring space echoing with conversation. Uncomfortable chairs were set on the black and white marble floor—most of them occupied. Despite his humbleness, Isabelle's father, Sir Edward Strathmore, was quite popular. Their botanical expedition to Tunisia last year, and triumphant return with an undiscovered flower, had fired London's imagination. Of course, the addition of bandits and exotic trappings had only served to inflame Society's interest.

No matter the subject, Sir Strathmore's lectures were not to be missed. Even if most of the attendees were consumed with discussing the events at last night's musicale. Isabelle caught snippets of theories raised, then dismissed. The air was rich with speculation: secret pickpockets, desperate men disguised as upstanding members of the gentry, quick-fingered maids. There seemed plenty of villains to choose from.

Isabelle, Richard, and their mother sat—as usual—in the front row. Isabelle idly pleated the folds of her blue muslin skirt and scanned the crowd, searching for a dour expression under black brows. If she were trapped in London, she might as well entertain herself with trying to search out the suspect she had glimpsed last night.

She spotted several black-haired young gentlemen, some of them looking to have just risen from their beds, but none were the man she recalled seeing at the musicale. She had nearly given up, when a figure beside the door caught her eye. Was that him?

"Excuse me, mother," Isabelle said, jumping to her feet. "I must visit the powder room."

"Do not tarry too long," Lady Strathmore replied. "Your father will be taking the podium soon."

Isabelle nodded and hurried toward the back of the hall. Sadly, by the time she pushed through the crowd and reached the place she'd spotted her suspect, he was gone. She couldn't spend more time searching. Perhaps after the lecture, she could coerce Richard into helping her look for the fellow. Brothers had to be good for something, after all.

She returned to her chair just as her father emerged from the back with his stack of notes. He brushed past the potted palms lining the wall, mounted the steps, and took his place at the mahogany podium. The crowd hushed in anticipation.

The lecture went splendidly—Sir Edward had a flair for storytelling and the ability to make his listeners feel immediately at ease. The applause afterward was long and genuine. Once it died down, the audience made a general surge toward the stage. Isabelle turned and beckoned to her brother, a surreptitious flip of her hand.

"We'll meet you at the back of the hall," she said to her mother.

Lady Strathmore nodded, continuing her conversation with a nearby friend.

"What?" Richard said when they were out of earshot.

"I saw someone, last night at the musicale," Isabelle said. "A tall man with black hair, a long nose, and a rather grim expression. He disappeared right after the ruby necklace was stolen."

"A suspect?" Richard grinned and raised his brows. "Marvelous. Shall we split up? I'll take the left side of the room."

"You wouldn't recognize him."

"At least I can find all the grim-looking black-haired men in that direction. Youngish, you say?"

"A bit older than us, but nothing like father's age. And I think he had a dark blue coat." She frowned, trying to coax more details from her memory.

"All right. Let's meet back here to compare notes in five minutes."

Isabelle glanced down at the silver watch pinned to her bodice, and nodded.

It was only three minutes later when a panicked cry rang through the hall. Isabelle hastened over to the knot of people in one corner, her boot heels clacking over the marble floor. A brown-haired young woman stood there, her face pale, surrounded by concerned onlookers. An older woman, her mother or chaperone, held her hand.

"It was my best bracelet," the young lady wailed. "Oh, I never should have worn it—but I did so want to show it off! The sapphires were lovely. And now it's gone forever. Stolen." She bit back a sob.

Another jewelry theft?

Isabelle glanced wildly around, but there was no sign of the black-haired man—if indeed it had been him she'd seen earlier. Across the rows of empty chairs, Richard met her eyes and shrugged.

Drat. It was hard to solve a mystery when the suspect proved so unobliging.

THE NEXT AFTERNOON, Isabelle coerced her brother into accompanying her on a bonnet-shopping expedition. At the fashionable heart of London, Bond Street was bustling with shoppers: a pair of ladies in striped silk walking dresses, their overburdened footmen scurrying behind with packages, a gentleman in a shockingly bright green coat and top hat, a pinch-faced governess escorting a flouncing miss. The noise of iron-bound carriage wheels over the cobbles vibrated through Isabelle, and the smell of fresh manure vied with the ever-present London soot.

"Aren't you finished yet?" Richard asked as she paused outside a milliner's shop. "You've purchased two bonnets and a hundred ribbons already."

"Eight ribbons," she replied, distracted by the front window display.

Were there actual hats underneath all those feathers and faux fruits? Cherries tumbled like a red waterfall over the brim of what would otherwise have been a quite fetching headpiece, and there was another hat so bedecked with vines and songbirds it would no doubt be attacked by falcons the moment the wearer stepped outside.

"We should buy Mother the one decorated with narcissus and chrysanthemum," her brother said. "Wouldn't that outrage Papa—spring and fall flowers mixed together? Ridiculous!"

"Papa thinks most hats are ridiculous. Still..." Isabelle smiled and turned toward the door of the shop.

From the corner of her eye, she glimpsed a shock of black hair beneath an elegant top-hat. Pausing, she took a second look. The man tilted his head, and recognition shivered through her. That long nose was unmistakable.

"Richard," she said, grabbing her brother's arm. "Up ahead. That's the man."

His brows shot up. "Hurry—we must keep him in sight."

Richard started off in pursuit. Isabelle hung on to his elbow, and he gave her an exasperated glance.

"Don't look like you're hurrying, for goodness sake," he said.

"Your legs are longer than mine, so I have to take quicker steps."

Still, Isabelle tried to lengthen her stride. They were keeping their quarry in sight, though they trailed him by half a block. The man moved with purpose, overtaking the more idle shoppers in his way. At the next corner, he made a sudden turn. By the time Isabelle and Richard reached the spot, he was gone.

"Damnation," Richard said, glancing to either side.

"Don't let Mother hear you swear." Isabelle scanned the street. "Look—there's a jeweler's shop near the end. Do you think he went in there?"

"It can't be that easy," Richard said. Nonetheless, he linked his arm with hers and tugged her down the cobbled street.

Isabelle gave her brother a quelling look. "Do attempt subtlety, Richard. I am shopping for a ring. No, perhaps a locket."

"One covered with diamonds?" His eyes lit. "An excellent plan. You be the bait. I'll lurk nearby and when the thief attempts to snatch the locket from your neck, I'll leap out and apprehend the fellow."

"Hm." She considered for a moment. "I'm afraid, even if we pool our money, we won't be able to afford anything nearly tempting enough. Did you see the size of those rubies that were stolen?"

Her brother let out a sigh. "Well, come along. At least we can see if the fellow's inside."

The jeweler's shop, despite being located just off the fashionable district, had a slightly ramshackle air. Richard opened the door for her, and Isabelle, heart knocking in her chest, stepped into the shop.

It smelled of silver polish and musty velvet. Ahead, a glass-fronted case held an array of snuff boxes, while a long counter to their left displayed jewelry: a few necklaces and bracelets, a lonely ring.

And there, leaning over the counter in deep conversation with the white-haired proprietor, was their suspect. She elbowed Richard in the ribs, then edged closer, trying to overhear.

"... on Saturday. It's of crucial importance—" The black-haired man broke off.

He sent her a glare, but there was something furtive about his eyes. His gloved hands balled into fists.

Isabelle dropped her gaze and attempted to appear innocent.

"Of course, my lord," the proprietor said. "It will not be a problem."

"Excellent. Then I bid you good day." Their suspect gave a sharp nod, then pivoted and brushed past them. The door closed firmly behind him.

It would be too obvious if they followed—especially since he'd gotten a good look at her.

"May I help you, Miss?" the jeweler asked, peering at her

through thick-lensed glasses that made his pale eyes appear small and watery.

"Have you any plain lockets?" she asked—though in truth, she wanted to demand if he had a necklace dripping with bright red rubies, or perhaps a sapphire bracelet.

Still, that would be a matter for the constabulary, provided she and Richard could give them more than guesses and speculation. She sighed and ran her finger along the edge of the case. A smudge of dirt marred the tip of her glove.

They were no closer to solving the mystery—and now she would have to buy an inferior bit of silver into the bargain.

Two days later, Isabelle sipped her over-sweet punch at the edge of Lady Roanoke's ballroom as the brightly-dressed crowd swirled past. A small orchestra played at one end of the floor, striving to be heard above the laughter and conversation, and the smell of various perfumes layered the air. She had danced all but two sets, and her dance card was filled for the rest of the evening. Luckily, Richard had agreed to waltz with her. She had no interest in being swanned about the floor by some sweaty-handed gentleman who fancied himself in love with her.

Love. She wanted nothing to do with the notion.

Wrinkling her nose, she set her punch aside and went to find the ladies' retiring room. So far, nothing exciting had happened at the ball. Still, the evening was not too far advanced. There could easily be another jewel theft—and this time she had no doubt she would recognize the black-haired man.

Imagine if she, Isabelle Strathmore, were able to identify the culprit! The constabulary would be so grateful. In fact, the queen herself might make a special mention of it. Smiling, Isabelle slipped out of the ballroom. It was cooler in the hallway, and quiet. The thick Persian runner cushioned her footsteps, and the intermittent sconces shed a calmer light than the brilliance in the ballroom.

Furtive movement caught her eye, and without a second thought, she slid behind a large fern potted in an oriental vase. Carefully, she peered between the fronds.

Partway down the hall, the Countess of Draymoor stood, stripping the rings from her gloved fingers. The woman glanced about, then snatched the glittering diamonds from her own throat and crammed them, and the rings, into her reticule. After a moment's hesitation, she tore the matching brooch off her blue silk gown and tucked it away. She tugged at her beautifully coiffed hair until it tumbled in disarray.

Then she opened her mouth wide, and screamed.

Isabelle clapped her hands over her ears as the woman's cry reverberated down the hall. An instant later, the main doors to the ballroom flew open, and several gentlemen hastened out. Behind them came their hostess and a number of women, voices raised in questioning alarm. Isabelle stepped out from her hiding place and joined the throng in the now-crowded hallway, confusion squeezing her thoughts.

Whatever was the countess up to?

"It was dreadful," Countess Draymoor said, one hand at her throat. "He leaped at me from one of the doorways, ripped off my jewelry, and ran before I could cry out for help."

"Which way did he go?" one of the gentlemen asked.

"What did he look like?"

"Was he a servant?"

"I...I think he went that way." The countess pointed away from the ballroom. "As to his form—he was large, and his hair was light in color—or so I recall. But I was so overset, you must understand...."

Three of the younger men immediately sprinted after the imaginary assailant.

"Give her some space," the mistress of the house said. "Come, Lady Draymoor, into the parlor. You have had quite a shock, and need to recover."

"Oh yes, please." The countess pressed a hand to her forehead. "I feel rather unwell."

Isabelle folded her arms and watched as Countess Draymoor was shepherded away. Now was not the time—but as soon as calling hours arrived on the morrow, she planned to pay the deceitful countess a visit.

It was fairly easy for Isabelle to convince her tender-hearted mother they should call upon Countess Draymoor.

"The poor woman," Lady Strathmore said as the footman handed her out of their carriage outside Lord Draymoor's town house. "How kind of you to suggest we pay her a visit —and the peonies are a lovely touch."

Isabelle dipped her nose into the bouquet she carried and inhaled deeply of the white flowers' delicate perfume.

"You know how father objects when they shed petals all over the conservatory floor," Isabelle said. "This way, there will be less for him to complain of."

And her sympathy made a convenient screen for her ulterior motive of questioning the countess. She mounted the curving granite steps leading to the front door. The brass knocker ring was heavy under her fingers.

A stoic-looking butler admitted them, taking their cards and indicating that the countess was receiving visitors in the Blue Room. A waiting footman bowed and ushered them in, and Isabelle handed the flowers off to him. The blooms would appear again in a few minutes, no doubt artfully arrayed in a cut-crystal vase.

The Blue Room was aptly named. Long velvet curtains, divans and settees, even the carpet on the floor was figured in tones of azure. The place seemed designed to highlight the cobalt of Countess Draymoor's eyes and set off her fair complexion.

Though it was an early hour for visitors, the countess was entertaining half a dozen ladies, seated in a semicircle in the center of the room. A quick scan of their faces proved that Isabelle knew none of them by name. Although the young woman with brown ringlets framing her face looked familiar —as did her older companion. A moment later, Isabelle caught her breath as belated recognition swept over her.

It was the young woman from the lecture hall, who had her bracelet stolen. Was she here to commiserate with the countess... or was something deeper at play?

"Lady Strathmore—please take a seat," the countess said, gesturing Isabelle's mother to a nearby chair. She made introductions, then turned to Isabelle. "And this is your lovely daughter, Isabelle, yes? I recall she came out earlier in the Season. Look at her hair, her eyes—such a beauty!"

Isabelle bobbed her head. It was not easy, acknowledging compliments when one was being spoken of in the third person. Wry humor sparked inside her. It had not escaped her notice that she and the countess were very similar in coloring. And she would wager it had not escaped the countess's, either.

Lady Strathmore sat, and Isabelle took the chair beside her—an overstuffed cushion of a thing that made her feel as though she were perched on a camel's hump. On her other side was a robust woman, who also looked vaguely familiar. Isabelle shot her a surreptitious glance. She was not entirely sure, but the lady resembled the woman whose rubies had been stolen at the musicale.

"We were just discussing the Queen's College," the countess said. "What do you think of the endeavor, Lady Strathmore?"

"The queen supports it, does she not?" Isabelle's mother said. "Surely our monarch's judgment is sound in such matters."

It was a clever answer, especially as neither Isabelle nor her mother were certain of the political leanings of this group. At home, of course, the family had discussed it. A school that intended to award academic qualifications to women? Society was abuzz. Detractors claimed that teaching higher mathematics to women would imperil their health, but the entire Strathmore family thought such claims ridiculous.

"I am relieved to hear you say so." A woman whom the countess had introduced as Lady Henrietta Stanley of

Alderley leaned forward, her dark eyes alight. "Surely, as a mother, you support the education of our young women."

"Indeed I do," Lady Strathmore said. "I understand the college is facing stern opposition from the Tories."

The countess let out a deep sigh. "My husband chief among them, I am saddened to admit. He is strongly against the idea of the college, and believes that education is of little use to a woman. Perhaps, if we'd had daughters instead of sons, he would feel differently."

"And perhaps not," Lady Stanley said, her voice brisk. "In any case, we all do what we can to support the worthy efforts of Mr. Maurice."

A charged silence fell, and Isabelle caught the jewel thief's 'victims' exchanging wary glances.

"Is Mr. Maurice accepting donations to his cause?" Isabelle asked, attempting to keep her voice casual. She smoothed the muslin of her skirts, the fabric cool under her hand.

"How thoughtful of you," the countess said. "Indeed, although one does not like to speak of it in polite company, the college is in serious need of funding."

Isabelle's heart sped, though she kept her voice calm. "I'm afraid I have very little to give. Except, perhaps..." She looked to her mother. "Might I give them one of grandmama's rings? I would like to donate some of my small inheritance in service to this worthy cause."

Lady Strathmore's eyebrows rose, but she nodded. "If you wish, then certainly you may. And I shall make sure to send a contribution as well."

Isabelle turned wide eyes to the countess. "I presume you

are able to accept donations that are not precisely in monetary form?"

"We will make do—and your generosity is sincerely appreciated." A delicate flush crept along the countess's cheeks, almost unnoticeable, unless one were watching for it.

Across from Isabelle, the young woman shifted, the fabric of her skirts making a hushing sound.

"Speaking of jewelry," Isabelle said, "I do want to offer my sympathy to you, Countess Draymoor. Whatever is London coming to, with this dreadful rash of necklaces being stolen so boldly off the necks of women?"

"It was a terrible shock," the countess said, one hand going to her chest. Around her, the other women nodded vehemently.

Isabelle was about to say something more, when a young man strode into the room. The words froze in her throat. It was the black-haired man!

"Charles!" The countess rose, a smile warming her features. "Do come in, my dear. Though I suppose you are only here in hopes of encountering Miss Shaw."

The young woman with the brown ringlets blushed.

"Mother, you know I enjoy your company," the young man said. His gaze went over the assembled ladies, then snagged on Isabelle. "I see you've made some new friends."

Countess Draymoor made the introductions, and an awkward silence settled. Isabelle's thoughts hummed. All the pieces were coming together—the false thefts, following Charles to the jewelry shop, the Queen's College need for funds in the face of serious opposition.

"Lady Draymoor," Isabelle said. "I hear you have a lovely

array of narcissus in your garden. Pray, would you show them to me?"

Her mother shot Isabelle a curious look, but the countess rose immediately.

"Of course. Being the daughter of a botanist, I imagine you are interested in such things. I prefer them for their scent, you understand. Ladies, please excuse us."

An attentive maid fetched Isabelle's pelisse, and a cloak for the countess, and together they went out into the rain-fresh garden. It was true, the beds were full of white and yellow blooms, but Isabelle paid no attention to the flowers or the sweet scent filling the air. She faced the countess, meeting the woman's blue eyes directly.

"My lady," Isabelle said. "Forgive me for speaking so directly—but you cannot continue your, shall we say, rather unorthodox method of raising funds for the college."

The countess arched one brow. "Are you saying you do not support such a worthy cause after all? I must admit, I am disappointed, Miss Strathmore."

"It's not that. Bluntly put, you must stop pretending that your jewelry is being stolen. You'll be caught—or your son will, as he attempts to sell supposedly stolen goods. Can't you see the danger?"

The countess turned her head and studied her rows of narcissus. After a moment she let out a quiet sigh. "How did you find out?"

"I saw you, last night. Saw you strip the gems from your fingers, and rip the brooch off your dress. Next time, it might be someone not so sympathetic."

"You must understand, it is the only way some of us have of supporting the college. I cannot ask my husband for money to give them—he would never yield to it. Yet it is essential Mr. Maurice succeed. If not for my generation, then for yours." There was a steely light in the countess's eyes. "I would 'steal' all my jewelry, if I could. It is the only thing of real value I can control."

Isabelle nodded. "Perhaps you could 'lose' some, instead. It's only a matter of time before Scotland Yard is called in."

"You are right—we must not be discovered." The countess pursed her mouth. "The jewel thief will have to disappear, leaving unsolved mysteries in his wake."

"I'm certain you'll find support in other quarters. I know my family will be able to give at least a small amount. Not every man feels as your husband does."

A shadow crossed the countess's face, quickly banished. "Thank you, Miss Strathmore. Now, do take a moment to breathe in the narcissus before we return to the house."

The sweet fragrance still caught in her senses, Isabelle and Countess Draymoor re-entered the Blue Room. Isabelle sat beside her mother, and the talked turned to inconsequentials. Soon thereafter, the Strathmores took their leave. Just outside the Blue Room was a side table holding a vase of the extravagant white peonies Isabelle had brought.

"I've always preferred flowers to jewelry," she said to her mother.

Lady Strathmore gave her a knowing smile. "Yes. And in my estimation, an education is worth even more than rubies."

She offered her arm. Isabelle took it, grinning, and together mother and daughter stepped out into the day.

∼

THE CLOCKWORK HARP

Miss Eleanora Thomas was not fond of the new instrument her mother had proudly installed in the drawing room three days earlier. It stood, a strange marriage of wood and metal, in the center of the plush Turkish carpet, directly in front of the bow window, where the harpsichord had used to reside.

Eleanora sat with her mother, Lady Thomas, on the plushly upholstered davenport, going over the day's correspondence. There were the usual invitations to parties and balls, all of which Eleanora was expected to attend. She would rather continue working on the new clockwork butterfly she was constructing than be paraded about on the Spring Season marriage mart, but as the eligible daughter of a viscount, she had little choice in the matter.

"Well!" Her mother held up a note decorated with scrollwork. "The Eldwins are holding a ball to celebrate their daughter Anne's engagement next week. We shall attend, of course."

An odd, barely audible hum emanated from the

soundbox of the harp. Eleanora glanced at her mother, but Lady Thomas seemed too engrossed in perusing her letters to notice the faint shimmer of sound.

Still, Eleanora slid a trifle closer to her mother and gave the instrument a sidelong look. The harp itself was unobjectionable. It was made of wood with gilt embellishments, strung with gut, and had a very pretty curve at the top. The ornately carved pillar was nearly as tall as Eleanora, who was admittedly on the petite side.

"So sad, about the younger sister," Lady Thomas continued. "But it's good to see families moving on. After an appropriate mourning period, of course."

The harp emitted another low sigh.

"Did you hear that?" Eleanora asked.

"I think you ought to wear your new gown," her mother said. "The one with the lifters. The style is all the rage, ever since the queen debuted it. Perhaps it will help you catch the eye of a worthy gentleman."

Eleanora was not particularly interested in catching the eye of a worthy gentleman. She suspected the unworthy ones were far more interesting. Sadly, at the advanced age of eighteen, she had little experience with members of the opposite sex, besides dancing and making desultory conversation with them. The things that truly interested her were not suitable topics for a young lady of good breeding.

Her parents, of course, did not know of her work. They thought the hours she spent in her room were passed in reading and painting watercolors of flowers, when in fact the watercolors were dashed out as quickly as possible so that she might fashion miniature clockwork creatures. Some day, perhaps, she would have a shop of her own, and a spacious workshop where she could construct all manner of fascinating things.

But not yet.

With an inaudible sigh, Eleanora turned her attention away from her impractical dreams and back to the harp.

She did not like the clockwork mechanism that had been attached to the instrument in order for it to play alone. It was an ungainly, spiderlike contraption folded beneath the harp. When wound with the large brass key, dozens of thin metal appendages would deploy. Each one was tipped with a tiny hook to pluck the string, and their striking put Eleanora in mind of an army of scorpions, stinging the music to life.

It was strange that she should find the mechanics so unsettling, for normally she was fascinated by clockworks. But there was something about the underbody of the harp that she disliked, beyond all reason.

She was glad when Lady Thomas declared them finished, giving Eleanora leave to adjourn from the drawing room. And despite the fact that her mother brushed her fancies aside, Eleanora thought there was something unnatural about the harp.

AFTER MIDNIGHT, the Thomas's townhouse lay still and slumbering. Eleanora woke, her mouth dry. Moving by feel, she went to the table where the water pitcher stood, but when she lifted it, she could tell it was empty. Drat it.

There was nothing for it but go down to the kitchen and fetch herself a glass of water. Her mother might insist on ringing for a maid, but Eleanora did not want to wake a sleepy serving girl from her well-earned rest. Then there would be two of them unhappily awake in the middle of the night, instead of just one.

Eleanora drew on her oriental silk wrapper, conveniently hung over the foot of her bed, and felt about for her lambskin slippers. When she could only locate one, she slid to her bedside table. She did not like the stink of sulfur matches, but even more she did not relish the thought of the cold kitchen flagstones under her bare feet.

The match flared, stinging her eyes with light and fumes. She quickly lit the candle in its holder and blew the match out. Her wayward slipper peeked out from the far corner of the bed, and with a sigh she retrieved it, picked up the candle, and slipped out into the hallway.

The flame sent eerie shadows dancing over the walls, and the air was cool and clammy. Drawing her wrapper closed with one hand, she hastened down the hall.

At the top of the staircase, she halted. Something was amiss. Holding her breath, she listened. Soft music drifted up from the drawing room.

Could one of the servants be awake, amusing themselves with playing?

It was a comforting notion, but the cold shiver along her spine told her otherwise. Especially as the plaintive notes were clearly the sound of a harp.

Pulse beating in the hollow of her throat, Eleanora crept down the stairs. She did not want to look into the drawing room—but she must. As she drew closer, she could almost make out the melody. Another step closer. Another.

The music stopped. Eleanora forced herself to hurry to

the open door of the room. She lifted her candle, hoping to catch whoever was playing.

Moonlight shone in through the bow window, bathing the harp in silver and shadow. The room was empty, except for the shapes of the pianoforte and harpsichord, the guitar in its stand, and the mandolin hung upon the wall. No servant girl leapt up, stammering apologies. No restless denizen of the house was present at all.

Swallowing the acrid taste of fear, Eleanora went over to the harp. She could not bring herself to touch it, but bent to study the mechanism. How could it have played, with no one to wind it?

It was possible the clockwork had not fully unwound from the last time her mother had demonstrated the mechanical harp to her admiring friends. Yet Eleanora distinctly recalled the music coming to a normal conclusion, ending with a ringing chord and the applause of the listeners.

She shivered and backed away, unwilling to take her gaze from the harp. Reaching the doorway, she slipped behind the shelter of the wall and took a deep breath.

It was only a midnight fancy; some melody lodged in her head that she had imagined hearing. That was all.

Mouth dry as parchment, she went to the sink and poured herself a cup of water. Through the windows, she could see the gaslights from the main avenue shining fitfully through the hedges. Overhead, the lit form of an airship drifted high above the London streets, blurred by fog into an elongated moon.

Certainly the clockwork had malfunctioned. Sometime in the next few days she would have the opportunity to examine it. Lord Thomas was away at Parliament most after-noons, and Lady Thomas would no doubt have some small social engagement Eleanora could beg off attending.

Young ladies of Quality were not taught to sully their hands with manual labor, and certainly not with grease and gadgets. But Eleanora had always had a fascination for the mechanical. She'd dismantled any number of her toys when she was a child, trying to determine what animated her clockwork animals and steam-driven calliope.

Her nurse had discouraged her, and hidden the broken evidence from Viscount Thomas.

"But what makes them go?" Eleanora remembered asking. "Have they a soul, like people do? Or are we clock-work inside, too?"

At that thought, she'd set her hand to her chest, wondering if she felt the whirring of gears or pumping of a steam engine. She had been told her heart resided beneath her ribs, but what, she wondered, powered it?

"They are just machines, and not for you to concern yourself over," Nurse had said, stuffing the remains of an eviscerated metal canary into the bottom of the rubbish bin. "Now, enough of this nonsense. If his lordship finds out, I'll be let go. And who will bury your toys then, miss?"

Eleanora had learned to keep her tinkering where her father could not see, but she had been delighted to find out there were people who studied such things.

"I would like to be an engineer," she'd announced at dinner one night, at the unfortunately innocent age of ten.

"What has that governess been teaching her?" Lord Thomas had said, setting his fork down with a clatter. "I'll have her removed immediately. Do endeavor to find her a more proper companion next time, Lady Thomas. If such a thing is within your capacity."

"Yes, dear," Lady Thomas had said, bending her head in acquiescence—but not before shooting Eleanora a look full of dire warning.

And so, sweetly indulgent Miss Tanager had been replaced by strict and stern Mrs. Corbin, and Eleanora closed her mouth, keeping her dreams and desires to herself.

For the next several years she'd comported herself like a lady—at least in public. At sixteen, she made her debut before the queen, and quickly learned how to make empty, convivial conversation at balls and parties.

In the last two years, however, she'd begun slipping out with only her maid in attendance and poking through the shops in the more questionable quarters of London. She loved the sooty, narrow streets where the clockmakers and steam engineers plied their trades, and the air was filled with whirring and buzzing and gouts of white, moist air.

It was there she had taken her pocket money and bought her first set of spanners. Later visits saw her returning home with gears and bits of bronze and copper wire concealed in her reticule. Her maid was loyal, and never said anything to Lord and Lady Thomas. Likely the woman knew she'd be summarily dismissed for not keeping Eleanora away from such places.

As if Eleanora would let anyone dissuade her from her passion.

The chill of the flagstones seeped through the soles of her slippers. She set her empty glass on the kitchen's wooden table and steadied herself for the journey back to her bedroom.

The downstairs remained silent except for the soft brush of her footsteps. She held her breath, her pulse accelerating as she approached the drawing room. Nothing stirred, no trickle of melody wended into the air. Still, the back of her neck prickled as she hurried past the open doorway. She did not feel safe until she had closed the door of her room behind her and turned the key, locking the door with a satisfactory thunk.

ELEANORA DID NOT HAVE a chance to tinker with the harp until four days later, when her mother went on an afternoon outing to bestow charity upon the orphans. Eleanora had stationed herself in the drawing room in case such an opportunity might arise.

"Are you quite certain you don't wish to accompany me?" Lady Thomas asked as she settled her cherry-decorated hat upon her upswept coiffure. "Lady Eldwin and her daughter will be coming, and it would do you good to cultivate their company."

"Perhaps next time," Eleanora said.

While they were acquainted, she'd never felt a particular resonance of fellowship with dark-haired Anne Eldwin. The girl had a dour disposition, her eyebrows always pinched together and a frown upon her mouth. Her younger sister, Belinda, had been much lighter of spirit—and fairer of coloring as well. The two sisters had been like night and day.

It was a tragedy that Belinda had drowned the summer before, in the lake near the Eldwin's country estate.

"Suit yourself," Lady Thomas said, with a sniff that indicated she would prefer it if Eleanora did no such thing, but instead bent to her mother's wishes.

"I shall be glad to remain at home." Eleanora gave her mother an unruffled smile. "Pay my regards to the Eldwins."

She continued sketching the pot of narcissus on the drawing room side table, pretending to be wholly engaged until her mother at last took her leave. Still, Eleanora scribed the trumpet-like shape of the flowers on the page until she heard the steam-carriage pull away, the iron-bound wheels rumbling over the cobbles.

She flipped the page of her sketch book, turning to the study she had made of the clockwork harp. It would come in handy, particularly if she dismantled any part of the instrument. Mother would not be pleased if her new instrument were broken.

Eleanora set her book down and pulled the spanner set from behind the divan's cushions, where she had earlier concealed it.

Despite her outward serenity, nervous energy ran just beneath her skin as she knelt before the harp. Carefully, she wound the key, then sat back as the spidery legs deployed and played a lively rendition of a Bach minuet.

The piece ended, the mechanism folded closed, and the harp was still once again.

Eleanora waited a full five minutes, but nothing further happened. Very well. She unrolled the canvas sheltering the set of tools and chose her second smallest wrench. She was not entirely certain about how to begin, but she felt more secure as her fingers wrapped around the solid metal.

Carefully, she rotated the harp so the back of the soundbox faced the window. Intermittent sun shone in, enough to illuminate the hollow inside of the harp through the oval holes set along the length of the instrument. The plucking mechanism was fastened to the outside of the box, but the gears that powered it were located inside. That must be where her answers lay.

Eleanora peered into the soundbox through one of the holes. The clockwork seemed perfectly fine at first glance. Held above the mechanism were a half dozen articulated arms, each one holding a thin metallic sheet with holes and bumps punched into the metal. Those must be the scores of the melodies the harp played, the pattern directing how the outer mechanism should strike the strings, like one would find inside a player piano.

Something glimmered at the bottom of the soundbox, something that resembled silk rather than metal or wood.

Frowning, she set her spanner down and rolled back the puffy sleeve of her gown. She did not relish the idea of reaching into the innards of the harp, but it was not as though the mechanism would bite. Clockwork could not hurt her.

She hoped.

With a deep breath to steady herself, she inserted her arm into the bottom hole of the soundbox. She could not see what she was doing, but let her fingertips glide over the teeth of the gears, then further down. She managed to fit her arm in just past the elbow, and continued to grope about.

At last her questing touch met a tangled softness. Her hand jerked away involuntarily at the impression she'd encountered a spider's nest, or something equally nasty. Gritting her teeth, she forced her fingers to close about the unsettling material.

She drew it out, her arm prickling as though some multi-legged creature were about to leap up and run along her skin. The instant her hand was clear of the harp, she dropped the object on the multi-colored carpet and rubbed vigorously at her forearm and fingers, trying to erase the sensation.

What lay on the carpet was not a creature of any kind. Eleanor leaned over to inspect it, still wary of touching the thing. It was a necklace woven out of golden fibers. An ornate braided flower in the center was decorated with a few pearls. The leafy fringe at the bottom was what she had first touched.

Gingerly, she poked at it. When the necklace did not move, she picked it up and studied it closely. It was, if she were not mistaken, woven of human hair.

Memorial jewelry made of the deceased's hair was quite fashionable, although why the necklace had been hidden in the bottom of the harp was a mystery. Even more disturbing: who was the dead woman whose hair made up the necklace?

"I don't believe in ghosts," Eleanora announced to the empty drawing room. "Particularly not ones who take up residence inside clockworks. The two are mutually exclusive."

Despite the firmness of her voice, however, she felt rather disquieted.

She tucked the necklace into the pocket of her morning gown. Perhaps with its removal, the harp would cease its uncanny playing. If it had ever actually done so, and the music had not been simply a figment of her imagination.

Briskly, she turned the harp back around. It seemed her spanners would not be needed, and she must put them away before her mother returned. She slipped her small wrench back into its pocket and re-rolled the canvas.

As she ascended the stairs, she heard the steam-powered carriage puffing and clattering up the street, bearing Lady Thomas home. Eleanora paused and glanced out the stairwell window, but it appeared the Eldwin ladies were no longer accompanying her mother.

Eleanora tucked her tools into their hiding place at the bottom of her wardrobe, along with the necklace, and met her mother in the front hallway.

"How were the orphans?" she asked.

"Ungrateful." Lady Thomas sniffed and pulled off her kid gloves. "You ought to have come."

"I will, when you next visit them," Eleanora said. "Shall we ring for tea in the drawing room?"

Lady Thomas did enjoy her civilized comforts. It would be no use questioning her until she was sufficiently recovered from her outing.

"That would be lovely. I need something to calm my nerves."

Some minutes later, the two of them sat on the davenport, the second-best silver tea service set on the table before them. Lady Thomas nodded to the maid when she brought a plate of biscuits, then poured out two cups of tea.

Eleanor stirred a lump of sugar into hers, then waited until her mother took a sip from the gold-rimmed cup and let out a sigh.

"I was wondering," Eleanora said. "Where exactly did you find the clockwork harp?"

At the time, she'd assumed her mother had purchased it from one of the instrument dealers she was fond of frequenting. In addition to the larger instruments in the drawing room, there were several flutes made of metal, wood, and bone, a mechanical snare drum (never used), and an antique lyre.

"It's quite the showpiece, I do agree," Lady Thomas said, glancing at the harp. "You know, I snatched it out from beneath Lady Eldwin's nose."

"Did you?" Eleanora set her teacup down.

Lady Thomas gave her a smug nod. "I was on High Street, and a steam omnibus had broken down, blocking traffic. A tinker in the most colorful cart was stopped there, and I saw the harp in the back. Of course, I immediately recognized it was a treasure."

"Of course."

"I asked the fellow if he would sell it to me, and he replied he was charged with delivering it to Lady Eldwin. I told him I would pay him double the commission. It did not take long for him to accept my coin, and move the harp into my carriage."

"Wasn't Lady Elwin upset?" Eleanora asked.

"She claims she knows nothing of any such instrument. Hmph. Clearly she was jealous of my coup, and did not want to admit it."

Eleanora gave the harp a long, considering look. If the instrument were somehow connected to the Eldwin family, then it was entirely possible the necklace she had removed from it was made of dead Belinda Eldwin's hair.

Why, then, did the family not know of the harp?

"Did the tinker say who had built the instrument?" she asked.

Lady Thomas waved her hand. "That minstrel mechanist

in Suffolk. He's rather well known, although the name escapes me at the moment."

"Tallesin," Eleanora supplied.

Indeed, if the harp had been built in his workshop, her mother had taken possession of a quite valuable instrument. Eleanora hoped it had not cost them too dearly.

She could not fault the workmanship; the ivory and pearl inlays on the top of the soundbox were exquisite, and the tone of the harp was sweet and true. It was only that the clockwork did not match the harp, and it perplexed her. Especially if it had come from the master minstrel's workshop.

"Yes, that's the name." Lady Thomas took another sip of tea.

"Isn't the Eldwin's summer estate in Suffolk?"

"Indeed. Which is why I believe Lady Eldwin is telling me untruths. I might have taken pity on her, had she actually confessed to commissioning the harp, but as it is..." Lady Thomas lifted her shoulders in a delicate shrug.

The maneuverings for position among the top ladies of the gentry generally were of little interest to Eleanora, but she suspected that her mother was incorrect in this matter.

"Speaking of the Eldwins, I trust your gown is in working order?" Lady Thomas asked. "The ball is in two days, after all."

"I will try it on now, but I'm certain the lifter mechanisms are well-tuned."

If they were not, she would simply tweak the lifters until her skirts floated about her like a cloud. It was an interesting fashion, and Eleanora did take some satisfaction in wearing something that was half contraption and half ball gown.

It was not until she was upstairs, with her wardrobe open, that she realized the harp had not made a single sound while they discussed its provenance, and the Eldwins. She glanced down at the drawer holding the necklace. If she returned it to its hiding place, would the harp begin its mysterious sighing once more?

She did not want to find out. Carefully removing her mechanized ball gown from the cedar-lined wardrobe, she closed the door, leaving the necklace and its secrets in darkness.

THAT NIGHT, Eleanora woke at the brush of a cold hand over her forehead. Heart pounding, she opened her eyes wide, searching the quiet shadows of her bedroom.

"Who's there?" she whispered.

No one answered, but the door of her bedroom swung open. Almost, she saw a ghostly figure of a girl in a long white dress outlined in the doorway. Eleanora rubbed her eyes. The vision was a product of dreaming, surely.

It took her several moments to gather her courage and slip out of bed to close the door. The wool rug was scratchy against her bare toes. She set her hand to the knob, then paused.

Faint music drifted down the hallway.

Curiosity warred with fear, and won. She snatched her wrapper and hastily donned her slippers, then went to the end of the hall. As she had known it would, the sound of a harp emanated from the drawing room.

The melody was plaintive and slow, and after a few bars

more, she recognized it as *Greensleeves*. Was that tune inscribed upon one of the metal cards inside the harp, or did ghostly fingers pull it forth from the harp?

Quietly, she descended the stairs. When she reached the bottom, the melody changed. It was another old ballad, and Eleanora hummed under her breath, trying to identify the refrain. *By the bonny mill-dams of Binoorie.*

A chill swept over her.

The harp was playing *The Cruel Sister*, a ballad recounting how a sister murdered her younger sibling by drowning.

"No," Eleanora whispered.

She did not want to know this. Belinda Eldwin's death was accidental. Surely her sister Anne had not pushed her into the lake.

Yet the image came to her of fair Belinda, her skirts dragging her down into the cold waters while she held out her hand to her sister, pleading for rescue.

Oh, why hadn't Lady Thomas left well enough alone! The harp intended to haunt the Eldwins had instead come to the wrong house. And Eleanora was even more convinced that Lady Eldwin was innocent of all knowledge of the cursed instrument.

A shiver wracked Eleanora while the notes of the ballad softly filled the air.

Why had Tallesin had fashioned the harp in the first place?

Perhaps the answer lay within the old ballad. Lord Thomas's library was well stocked, and she knew where the collections of folklore and ballads were shelved.

Unfortunately, she would have to pass the drawing room to reach the library.

Clutching her wrapper tightly closed, she crept down the wide hallway. Fear clogged her throat, but as soon as she reached the open drawing room door, the music stopped.

Eleanora forced herself to look in. There was no moon, just fog outside the bow window. The harp stood alone, each string faintly outlined in a pale glimmer.

She had to swallow twice before she could speak.

"I will try to help you," she said, softly. Though she did not know how she would accomplish it.

There was no acknowledgement, no chord of thanks or ghostly form materializing to make her a bow. The light faded from the harp, until it was a shadow silhouetted against the gray fog.

Slowly, Eleanora's heartbeat returned to normal. She took a deep breath, then continued on to the library.

Banked coals in the fireplace glowed red. She lifted one of the mantelpiece candles and bent to light it from the coals, welcoming the heat against her hands and face. The wick flared to life, and she squinted against the sudden brightness.

A few minutes' searching yielded up the thick tome titled *Collected Ballads of Scotland and the North*. The gold lettering on the cover gleamed in the candle light. Eleanora paged through until she found what she was seeking: *The Cruel Sister*. She skimmed the text, fingers growing colder as she read.

She had remembered it correctly; the ballad recounted the tale of two sisters, one fair, one dark. A knight came to court the eldest, but instead fell in love with the younger sister. Consumed with jealousy, the dark girl threw her sister into the sea and refused to help her as she drowned. All of that was terrible enough, but the end of the ballad made Eleanora's heart freeze.

> *A minstrel walked along the strand,*
> *And saw the maiden float to land.*
> *He made a harp of her breastbone,*
> *Whose sound would melt a heart of stone.*

That would explain Tallesin's involvement, though why he would build a harp out of a dead girl's body, she could not fathom. In truth, the instrument was mostly made of wood. But the ivory inlays took on new meaning. She shuddered, and continued reading.

> *He took three locks of her yellow hair,*
> *And with them strung the harp so rare.*

The harp was not strung with hair, but with sinew. Eleanora most emphatically did *not* want to think about where it had come from. The hair necklace hidden inside the soundbox fulfilled that role well enough.

Hair, and bone, and sinew. It explained why removing the necklace had not kept the harp from playing. There was enough of Belinda Eldwin in the instrument to anchor her ghost.

> *He took it to her father's hall*
> *To play the harp before them all.*
> *But when he placed it on the stone*
> *The harp began to play alone.*

And that was where the plan had gone awry. The harp was not in the dead girl's home—though it certainly played alone.

The ballad went on to describe how the harp sang of the girl's murder, and, in tears, the elder sister confessed.

Well then.

Eleanora closed the book and stared absently at the flickering candle flame. It was clear she must convince Lady Thomas to take the harp to Anne Eldwin's betrothal ball. Appearances meant everything to her mother. Lady Thomas was proud and possessive, but she could be talked into showing her generosity of spirit by giving Anne Eldwin the harp as a wedding gift.

And once there, Eleanora only hoped the harp would perform as described.

THE ELDWIN'S ballroom shone brightly, illuminated by crystal-bedecked gaslight chandeliers hanging from the tall ceiling. Light glittered off gemstones fastened about throats and arms—rubies and diamonds, emeralds and sapphires, sending glints of color over the gaily-dressed throng.

The air was sweet with mingled perfumes as Eleanora followed her mother across the polished marble floor to where the Eldwins stood on a dais, greeting their guests. The skirts of her gown billowed and floated about her like a gossamer cloud, the lifter mechanism expanding into empty space and pulling back when she got too near any object.

Behind them, a footman carried the harp, draped in a blue silk cloth. Eleanora bit her lip, her heart sinking. What if she had been wrong? Haunted midnight melodies now seemed the product of her own fevered imagination.

The noisy, well-lit ballroom was a bastion of normalcy. Even if there were a ghost, she would not materialize in such a place.

"My dear Lady Eldwin, Lord Eldwin," Eleanora's mother said as they arrived at the foot of the dais. "Our most sincere congratulations to your daughter, Anne, upon her betrothal."

Dark-haired Anne, standing beside her mother, nodded, her face unsmiling. At her other side, her betrothed, Sir William Hunt, looked a bit glum as well.

Lady Eldwin inclined her head in thanks. "I see you have brought us a gift. How kind."

"Yes." Lady Thomas gave her an insincere smile. "I thought it only right, in the spirit of friendship, to bestow this fine instrument upon Miss Anne."

She beckoned to the footman, who set the harp down on the marble floor and pulled the silk cloth off with a flourish. Eleanora watched closely, but none of the Eldwins showed any flash of recognition—or fear—at the sight.

"How very cunning," Anne Eldwin said. "Does it play?"

"Of course it plays." Lady Thomas sniffed, then looked at Eleanora. "Do wind it, my dear."

Heart thumping, Eleanora bent and turned the brass key three times around.

Nothing happened.

The Eldwins' looks of expectation turned to boredom.

"Play," Eleanora whispered, turning the key again.

One of the spidery legs jerked, then fell off, landing on the marble with a metallic ping. Some of the nearby guests laughed.

"A pity it's not in working order," Lady Eldwin said. "I suppose it can go in the back parlor as a curiosity." She turned her gaze to the next guests in line, clearly dismissing Lady Thomas and her gift.

"Wait!" Eleanora cried.

Impulsively, she pulled one of her hairpins free. She scooped up the leg and deftly re-attached it, bending her hairpin to help hold the appendage in place.

The clockwork instantly sprung into motion, plucking out a sweet waltz. From the corner of her eye, Eleanora saw a tall, white-haired gentleman push through the crowd. He stared at the harp with a look comprised equally of relief and revulsion.

The waltz slowed, and as it did, the lights began to dim. Lord Eldwin commenced chiding his wife about not taking proper care of the chandeliers, but he fell silent as a chilly blast of air swept through the ballroom. The mechanism folded itself beneath the soundbox of the harp, yet the instrument continued to play. *The Cruel Sister* rang out, and Anne Eldwin's sallow skin turned pale.

The lyrics of the ballad echoed in Eleanora's mind.

The first string sang a doleful sound:
"The bride her younger sister drowned."

Whispers of consternation rose from the assembled guests, all attention drawn to the front of the dais. The harp was beginning to glow, bluish-white light outlining the strings and pouring from the soundbox, where Eleanora had replaced the hair necklace.

Lady Eldwin took a step back, her eyes wide, but her

daughter seemed frozen in place. A single tear slipped down her cheek. Then another. Beside the harp, a figure coalesced —a young woman with long, flowing hair, gowned in white. Slowly, she raised her hand and pointed at Anne Eldwin.

"No!" Anne cried, her voice filled with terror. Tears glazed her face.

Beside her, Sir William Hunt stared at the ghost, love and longing clear in his expression.

"Belinda," he whispered.

The glowing figure nodded, once. A cold wind whipped about the ballroom, jangling the crystals on the dim chandeliers and blowing skirts wildly about.

Quickly, Eleanora deactivated the mechanical lifters of her gown to keep it from twisting and billowing. The white-haired gentleman moved to stand beside her, his gaze fixed on the ghost.

"She will have her vengeance at last," he murmured.

The wind died down to an icy breath, and quiet filled the emptiness it left behind. The ghost of Belinda Eldwin glided toward her sister, until they stood face to face. Mirrored dark and light, alive and dead.

Slowly, the dead girl raised her hand and pointed at her sister.

"I pushed her in," Anne Eldwin sobbed. "Belinda—oh, I am so sorry!"

For still moment, the ghost of Belinda Eldwin regarded her murderer. Then, with a sigh, the glowing figure walked right through the living flesh of her elder sister.

Anne let out a harrowing shriek and fell to the floor. Sir William went to one knee beside his betrothed and took her wrist.

"She has fainted," he said after a moment. "Someone, fetch smelling salts."

Eleanora noted that he let go of the young lady's wrist rather quickly and wiped his fingers on his trousers, his expression veering into loathing.

As the lights brightened, Lady Elwin regarded the harp, her face twisted with despair.

"Take it away!" she cried, then turned, weeping, into her husband's shoulder.

Conversations sprang up all over the ballroom, loud and speculative. Eleanora felt overcome with sadness. Justice had been served, surely, but she had not enjoyed her part in it.

"Who are you, sir?" she asked, catching the arm of the white-haired gentleman.

"My name is Tallesin Woodweft," he said.

"But... you are the minstrel mechanic who made the harp." Eleanora studied his lined face, his faded blue eyes.

"Indeed, to my sorrow. A sad tale, that."

"Perhaps you might tell me. Some time, under better circumstances."

He nodded and handed her his card. "You seem a sensible young lady. Do write—I feel we might have a beneficial future correspondence."

"I shall." She tucked the card into her reticule.

With a weary nod, he turned and beckoned to one of the nearby footmen.

"I shall remove this cursed harp," the minstrel said. "Convey it to my carriage."

The footman hesitated, then, at an impatient gesture from Tallesin Woodweft, lifted the instrument. As he hefted it into his arms, the clockwork structure disengaged from the base of the harp and fell to the marble floor with a metallic clatter. The footman started violently and dropped the instrument.

"No," Tallesin cried, lunging forward as Eleanora rushed to help.

Too late. The harp shattered, bits of wood flying. The strings snapped from the soundbox in a cacophony of discord, and in that sound, Eleanora heard the last cry of an unearthly voice.

The noise silenced the guests once again, and they moved far back from the ruined harp lying in the middle of the ballroom: cracked wood and tangled strings, splintered inlay, and the pale weave of a dead girl's hair.

~*~

THE PERFECT PERFUME

She had not meant for her concoction to explode.

Charlotte Barrington buried her nose in her sleeve and took a step back from the smoking vial on the laboratory table. A spark flew from the vial and singed a hole in her poplin skirt. Despite her goggles, her eyes burned. *Damnation.*

She was missing some essential component. None of the normal stabilizers were effective—and she certainly could not have her perfume exploding.

Perhaps it was the pinch of golden dust she had added, advertised as *Genuine Powdered Unicorn Horn*. The small cobalt jar had cost more than she could afford—but she was desperate to find the unique ingredient that would secure her commission as Parfumier to the Queen.

Several perfume makers were vying for that title, to be bestowed during Victoria II's upcoming Silver Jubilee celebration. It was Charlotte's last chance to preserve her parents' legacy, to prove that, despite all assertions to the contrary, she *could* carry on the name of Mlle Violetta, Parfumier Extraordinaire.

To do so she must take reckless chances.

Three days. That was all the time remaining until her appointment with the queen. Before then, Charlotte must discover the unique ingredient that would make her perfume not just a scent, but an *event*.

She had observed in the laboratory how some substances took on curious properties when viewed through restricted spectrums of light. Her goal was to formulate an elegantly refreshing perfume that, when combined with a dark glass filter, created a spectacular effect about the wearer. A silver glow, in honor of the queen's twenty-fifth year of reign.

It was an ambitious, some might say impossible, endeavor.

At first, Charlotte had tried incorporating traces of precious metals into her perfumes: silver, platinum, white gold. While some of them created a faint opalescence, none of them reacted under lights, no matter the spectrum applied.

Saffron and exotic spices likewise proved invisible, as did all botanicals. She soon moved into experimenting with odd and rare ingredients: powdered peacock egg, ground malachite, distilled virgin's tears, soot from burnt silk, persimmon seeds. Powdered unicorn horn.

None of those had been effective. But at least she had achieved a lovely explosion.

She rang for her maid. "Hetty, we are going out."

In addition to Hetty, she would bring along one of the burlier footmen. Ben, perhaps. There was one last place she had not yet tried. Dante's Diabolical Diversions, an unsavory shop at the edge of the Seven Dials district

"Shall I have the driver ready the carriage?" Hetty asked.

Charlotte tapped her lips with one finger. The squalid alley housing Dante's was not a locale frequented by the upper gentry, and she wanted her visit there to go unnoticed. Not to mention that announcing the presence of wealth in the worst slum in London was hardly wise.

"No," she said. "We do not wish to call attention to ourselves, and there's no good place for the carriage to wait. We shall take the omnibus. Now, fetch my black cloak—the wool, not the satin-lined."

Hetty brought the cloak, and her gloves and hat, and a gorgeously ruffled parasol that Charlotte left propped beside the door. An afternoon in the June sun would not damage her complexion beyond repair, especially if she wore her new top hat. She donned the hat, tucking up a stray curl of her dark hair, and surveyed herself in the hall mirror. Upon consideration, she removed the lavender-dyed ostrich feather from the hatband. It was entirely too remarkable.

Once outside the sheltering walls of Barrington House, the screeches and smells of London assaulted her senses. Charlotte wrinkled her nose as they went down the street. Rotting garbage mingled with horse manure, coal smoke, and the tang of sulfur. Some days she cursed the gift of her superior sense of smell.

Soon enough, though, her nose became numbed. She and Hetty, trailed by the reliable Ben, made their way past the summer-green of Hanover Square and over to Oxford Street.

"Hail a cab, mistress?" Ben inquired, nodding at one of the horse-drawn conveyances.

"No, we shall take the omnibus. Here it comes."

The plume of steam was unmistakable, a white billow announcing the omnibus's route. They might be no less conspicuous, but it would be easier to blend in with the crowd and slip off when they reached their destination.

The bus lurched to a halt as Ben flagged it down, the driver operating the levers and brake. Two dandies rose and offered Charlotte and Hetty their seats. Charlotte heard her maid muffle a laugh the gentlemen's ostentatious clothing. The chartreuse stripes on one of the gentleman's coats clashed horribly with his scarlet waistcoat, while the second fellow sported a bright orange necktie done up in a puffy, cascading bow. *The Andrew*, she believed the style was called, named after Victoria II's eldest son.

The omnibus carried them out of Mayfair and into the streets that marked the beginning of Seven Dials. Charlotte tapped Hetty on the arm and caught Ben's eye.

When the conveyance halted to admit a pair of laundresses, the three of them slipped off. Under cover of the plume of steam, Charlotte drew them back against the stained brick of a nearby building. Satisfied no one was following, she nodded to her companions, then led the way down a side street.

They darted across another well-trafficked street and fetched up at the mouth of an alley.

"Odhams Walk, mistress?" Ben peered dubiously into the dank recess.

"Indeed." Charlotte kept her tone brisk, though the back of her neck prickled.

Perhaps it had been a mistake to come. Regardless, she must make the best of it. If the missing ingredient for her perfume was to be found, she could not let squeamishness stand in her way.

"Come along," she said. "Watch your step."

The light faded as they progressed, with only a slice of cloud-studded sky overhead providing illumination. Nasty things were strewn in the alley, things she had no wish to examine more closely. Grateful for her well-made boots, she stepped over them and skirted the noxious puddles. Ben, expression grim, took Hetty's arm. He would have taken Charlotte's but she had made it clear in the past that she needed no such assistance.

After passing three weathered doors, she halted. Although Odhams Walk was mostly residences—no doubt overcrowded and unsanitary—the window beside her bore lettering in chipped white paint. *Dante's Diabolical Diversions.*

She had been there twice before—years ago, and in the company of her father. Charlotte squared her shoulders, then lifted the black knocker on the door and gave three taps. The knocker left a smudge on her white gloves.

After a long minute with no response, Ben shuffled his feet.

"Nobody's home," he said, glancing up and down the alley. "Best we leave now, mistress."

Hetty remained silent, her eyes wide, her grip tight on Ben's arm.

"Not yet." Charlotte tapped thrice more.

This time, footsteps sounded. Slowly the door opened, bringing a waft of dry air scented with ylang-ylang. A tall, thin man stood at the threshold, his black hair slick with macassar oil. His prominent nose overshadowed thin lips that looked as if they did not often take the shape of a smile.

"Mr. Dante," Charlotte said. "May we come in?"

He looked her up and down, then flicked a glance at Ben and Hetty.

"Certainly, Miss Barrington. Please, enter." His voice was low and sonorous, and echoed strangely. She suspected him of using some kind of device to enhance the effect.

Dante stepped back and opened the door, and she and her companions hastened inside. Despite her apparent calm, Charlotte had felt the watching eyes as her party lingered overlong in the rank alley of Odhams Walk. Another minute or two, and they would have had to fend off thieves, or worse.

"I was sorry to hear of your parent's tragic airship accident," Dante said. "I understand you are attempting to continue the Parfumerie by yourself?"

His tone held disbelief that she would succeed in doing so; a sentiment echoed by most of the gentry.

"I am running the business," she said, her voice resolute.

It had been nearly a year since her parents had died while searching the South Pacific for exotic ingredients. Charlotte folded one arm across her stomach. She did not think she would ever recover from the searing pain of their loss.

And now she had run out of funds. Her uncle, Lord Barrington, had been generous to a point, but his patience was growing thin. There was only so far he would go to assist the daughter of his flighty younger brother. Soon she would be seeking employment as a governess or lowly lab assistant, her dreams—her legacy—smashed like broken perfume bottles at her feet.

"Scrumptious!" a harsh voice called.

Hetty gasped, and Charlotte jumped, just a little. She had

forgotten the clockwork myna bird Dante kept in his shop. Ebony-feathered, it hopped down from a stack of dusty books and surveyed them, head cocked. It looked quite real, but for the large brass key set in its back.

"What may I do for you this afternoon?" Dante asked, a hint of morbid amusement in his tone. "I do not flatter myself by thinking this is a courtesy call as you passed through the neighborhood."

Charlotte lifted her chin, projecting a confidence she did not feel. "I would like to see your most exotic ingredients."

"Indeed. Dare I ask what it is you are attempting to formulate, Miss Barrington?"

"Salubrious!" they myna screeched.

"Nothing in particular," Charlotte said. "I am conducting a small experiment."

Dante paused. When she did not elaborate, the corner of his mouth curled up in the beginnings of either a smile or a sneer.

"I believe the contents of this case will interest you." He led her past the skeleton of a fanged feline, around a huge marble urn holding a bouquet of colorless hydrangeas, and to a gleaming mahogany display case. A gasolier in the shape of an inverted lotus hung directly above, casting a clear light over the contents.

Through the glass top she could see an array of fascinating items. She leaned forward, her gloved fingertips resting on the glass.

"What is that bright red liquid in the vial?" she asked.

"Distilled venom from the coral cobra, found exclusively in deepest India."

"And the blue granules?"

"Tears of Amariko, formed when molten stone meets the ocean. They can only be gathered twice a year at lowest tide, on a remote Oriental island."

"And that?" She slid one gloved finger to the upper right corner, where a shimmering stone lay in a small velvet-lined box. Against the burgundy velvet, the stone shone nearly silver—a pearly gem that one moment resembled hematite, the next pure opal.

"That, my dear girl, is starstone."

Charlotte slanted a look up at him. She had never heard of such a thing.

"Fallen from the sky," Dante said, "in a glittering flash of silver. Would you like to hold it?"

"Is it... dangerous?"

He let out a sharp bark of laughter. "A bit of wisdom hides behind those pretty blue eyes of yours. You may handle the stone with no ill effects."

Dante rounded the case and slid open the back panel. Withdrawing the box containing the stone, he held it out to her.

Carefully, Charlotte touched it with one gloved finger. It was not hot, nor did anything spark or flare at the contact. She took the stone—no bigger than a quail's egg—between her forefinger and thumb, then nearly dropped it again from the unexpected weight.

"Ah yes," Dante said. "I should have warned you it was heavy."

She had the impression he was laughing at her, though no mirth escaped his still features. The stone weighed as much as a piece of lead three times its size. Perhaps the proprietor was telling the truth, and it had indeed fallen from the heavens.

"How much?" She attempted to keep her voice nonchalant. She did not think she succeeded.

"Sarsaparilla!" the myna called from directly behind her.

Charlotte jerked, her movement causing the gaslight to dance in broken reflections over the starstone.

"Careful." Dante waved the box and, reluctantly, she deposited the stone back on the velvet. "How much, indeed? I could ask no more than twenty-five gold pieces."

Hetty let out a gasp, and Charlotte blinked.

"That is a large sum," she said. "I am not certain I can pay so much."

"But your uncle can." Dante leaned forward. "Send that brute of a footmen back with the money, and I will give him the starstone."

"I—"

"Send him, and three of his friends. This is not the most savory of neighborhoods. I fear you might have lingered overlong, Miss Barrington. I would not want you to come to any... harm."

At this, Dante did smile, an expression Charlotte would have been just as happy to miss.

"We will be off, then," she said. "Expect Ben—and his friends—to call upon you later this afternoon."

"Not too late," Dante said, ushering them to the door. "Seven Dials at dusk is not safe for even four intrepid servants."

Ben glanced at her, throat moving in an unhappy swallow.

"Then we had best make haste," she said. "Good day, sir."

She motioned her companions over the threshold, and they hastily complied. As Dante shut the door behind them, she heard the mynah yell once more.

"Sedition!"

"What a nasty bird," Hetty said. "And man, and shop. Please, promise we shall never visit again, mistress."

Charlotte patted her arm (which was not a promise) and marched down Odhams Way. Though the skin between her shoulder blades prickled, she refused to look behind her. Anyone watching would receive no satisfaction from seeing her unease.

Upon their return to Barrington House, she went directly to her uncle's study to plead her case.

"Twenty-five gold pieces! Do you think I'm made of money, girl?" He scowled, his monocle glinting with reflected gaslight from the lamp in the corner.

She twisted her fingers in the smooth silk of her skirt. "This is the final ingredient, I'm sure of it."

"Your hobby is growing bloody expensive." He picked up the glass of scotch sitting on his desk and took a long swig.

Charlotte said nothing. Lord Barrington did not like beggars.

He replaced his glass on the cluttered desk, between the gem-encrusted monkey skull and the tiny automaton of a ballet dancer. Charlotte disliked the clockwork figure. It was an older model, and despite being wound at regular intervals was unpredictable. For days the dancer would stand there, unmoving, staring with painted glass eyes at nothing. Then it would suddenly burst into motion, twirling *en pointe* and performing manic *grande jetes* that scattered the papers across the carpet.

"Well then," her uncle said. "If you are so certain, I expect repayment. With interest."

"That will be amenable," she said, though her stomach churned at the prospect of failure.

"Then send Ben in, and I will see to procuring this ingredient of yours. You do understand this is the last time I will aid you, do you not?"

She gave him a tight, dry smile. "I understand."

So much depended upon the starstone.

She dropped her uncle a curtsey, then retreated to her laboratory. Who knew how much longer she would have that luxury? Her future was a dark sky—no moon, no stars to navigate by. Only hope. And the tremendous weight of fear.

If she lost the Parfumerie, she lost everything.

Two hours later, Ben knocked at the laboratory door and delivered the starstone, encased in its velvet-lined box. After Charlotte sent him away, she held the heavy box and pondered. So very much rode on the contents. How was she to incorporate the starstone into her perfume?

The laboratory was equipped with a crushing machine, yet she felt reluctant to consign the stone to its jaws. Moving on a hunch, she instead went to the large teardrop-shaped copper boiler in the corner.

She opened the small bulb on top of the steamer, careful not to dislodge the copper pipe that snaked from the top. Inside its box, the starstone gleamed even more brightly than she recalled, as if lit with interior radiance.

Though not given to such things in general, she whispered a small prayer, then set the starstone on the metal grating of the upper bulb. The lower portion of the distiller was filled with fresh water, specially transported to London from Seven Springs; the source of the Thames River, unsullied by soot or effluvium.

She closed the bulb, then lit the ring of gas flames beneath the boiler. The fire, blue shading to yellow, licked at the rounded copper underside. Overhead, the tube snaked the length of the laboratory, ending at the glass apparatus of the *essencier*.

Charlotte considered the still. Oh, she was a fool to think she could extract anything from a *stone*. Almost, she flung open the bulb and snatched the starstone, consigning it to the jaws of the pulverizer.

But she had learned to heed her instincts. She would let the process work for three hours, then check the *essencier*. Meanwhile, she would turn her attention to the rest of the perfume components.

The tall clock in the corner ticked off the seconds as she bent over her work table. Light from the mullioned windows high overhead filtered through her vials and bottles of oils, ranging in color from palest honey to an indigo the color of midnight. She had no need of belladonna for this concoction, however.

Using tiny pipettes, she placed her chosen scents in a small glass bowl. Three drops of balsam, the freshness balanced by two drops of tea rose. Then the too-feminine result smoothed by a drop of chamomile, and her signature —a single drop of violet essence.

Violet was the most complex of the floral scents, due to its singular property of temporarily stealing the sense of smell. With judicious use, however, even the simplest of perfumes could become ever-engrossing; tantalizing the nose, then retreating, only to return again in a waft of awareness.

Her mixture was not yet complete. The addition of ambergris for the fixative added a particular, musky component that attracted men and women alike. Charlotte measured the smoky brown oil, then stirred the contents of the bowl with a long glass wand. It was far too strong. Six parts of diluent would follow, the alcohol she made herself when the still was not otherwise engaged.

A pity she had to keep the diluent locked in the cabinet, but after one of the scullery maids had stolen a bottle, Charlotte took extra precautions. She shuddered at the waste. Imagine, drinking the highly-refined liquor she had worked so hard to produce. The reverse alchemy of the human body would transmute the liquid back into something far more base.

"Miss Charlotte?" Hetty's voice sounded from the speaking tube mounted beside the door.

"Yes?"

"If you're free, it's time to dress for dinner. I've laid out your green taffeta gown. Does that suit?"

Charlotte cast a glance at the distiller, which seemed to be boiling merrily away. According to the clock, she had been in the laboratory a little over an hour.

"Very well. I shall be up shortly."

Preparing for dinner, and the meal itself, should while away another hour or more. It would prove distraction enough from the question of whether the starstone would yield up its essence.

In truth, dinner took nearly two hours, due to the presence of Lord Barrington's favorite guest. Sir John Holcomb was an inventor, and his thoughts on simulacra and automatons were always fascinating. Only a half-decade older than herself, Charlotte was usually more than happy to spend time in his company. His face was handsome enough, but it was the quickness of his mind that most engaged her.

Still, she could not help peeking at her pocket watch at regular intervals.

At last her uncle folded his napkin and set it on the table.

"You are welcome to join us for an after-dinner aperitif, Charlotte," he said. "However, I have the sense you are eager to return to your laboratory."

"Have you a thrilling experiment brewing?" Sir Holcomb leaned forward, interest flashing in his hazel eyes.

"Perhaps." She smiled, but said nothing more.

Of all her acquaintances among the gentry, Sir Holcomb was the only one who had never expressed doubt that she could carry on her parent's legacy as London's premier parfumiers. Still, she did not want to speak of what she was attempting. The chance of failure lay too close, like a noose waiting to tighten about her neck.

When she took her leave of the gentlemen, they were already embroiled in a lively discussion about the advances in self-guided airships.

Her heartbeat thumped more loudly than her footsteps over the thickly patterned hall carpet as she headed toward the laboratory. Despite her hopes, she knew that stones did not contain oils. She was a fool to think otherwise.

The quiet hiss of the gaslights filled the laboratory as Charlotte hurried to check the still. She slid back the small door on the upper bulb and peeked at the starstone. It appeared darker, but that might owe more to being saturated with moisture than to any distillation of its radiance.

Biting her lip, she followed the copper tubing to the glass chamber of the *essencier*. The glass cylinder was partially filled with water, the hydrosol of any extraction. In the usual course of distillation, the essential oils would be floating, lighter than the water below.

There was no substance lying above the hydrosol.

Charlotte's anticipation clicked to a stop, like a clockwork device left unwound. The process was a failure.

The sour taste of defeat filled her mouth as she turned away.

Something caught her eye, glimmering at the bottom of the vessel. She whirled, taffeta skirts rustling as her hopes began ticking again. A silvery substance lay beneath the water, metallic and otherworldly-looking; somewhat akin to liquid mercury

Of course! The starstone's essence was not lighter than water—it was heavier. Charlotte tipped her face up to the distant, invisible sky in thanks. Relief eased her breath, sweetened her blood.

Still, it would not be an easy task to obtain the starstone essence from the vessel. The glass cylinder was constructed to pour oils off the top. Instead, she needed to remove as much of the water as possible, without disturbing the essence, in a sort of reverse-process.

Droplets continued to fall into the *essencier* from the copper tube overhead. She leaned forward and studied one. It looked perfectly clear as it slid down the narrow opening of the vessel to meet the water below.

Her goggles lay nearby. Donning them, she bent until her

eyes were level with the hydrosol, then adjusted her lenses to their maximum magnification.

The next drop slithered into the hydrosol. It was pure, with no hint of brightness occluding the water. She crouched and looked up through the liquid, but could see no trace of essence floating downward.

It appeared the starstone had been sufficiently extracted. She pushed her goggles to the top of her head, ignoring the way they mussed her coiffure. Appearances were one thing, but this experiment was of paramount importance. Certainly, she might change out of her gown, but she simply could not wait. The cupboard held a number of large aprons, and sturdier gloves than her silken evening ones.

Once she was better garbed for laboratory work, Charlotte shut off the boiler and closed the condensing tube. She removed the starstone back to its velvet-lined box, noting that the distillation process had not reduced its unusual weight.

Walking carefully, so that her footsteps did not disturb the concoction inside the *essencier*, she fetched a large glass ladle and bowl. She lifted the top of the vessel and began ladling out the hydrosol. Who knew what properties that water held? Unlike rose or lavender water, she did not think it would have a salubrious effect upon the skin.

Slowly, slowly, she skimmed the water out of the *essencier* until the ladle dipped perilously close to the starstone essence. Evaporation would have to do the rest, but she could not risk the turbulence of boiling.

It made her want to stamp her feet with impatience. *So close!*

She might be able to draw out a small amount of the

substance, though—enough to mix with her test perfume. Resolutely, she pulled her goggles back on and decreased the magnification to normal.

With her longest pipette, Charlotte succeeded in capturing a few drops of the starstone essence. She carried it carefully to her work table. Holding her breath, she let a single drop fall into the bowl containing her perfume.

She could not help flinching back as the essence reached the mixture—but this time there was no explosion. Indeed, a faint, sweet scent drifted from the bowl. Charlotte sniffed. It was her perfume, certainly, but with an ethereal note even her trained nose could not identify.

The true test would be whether or not the perfume reacted beneath filtered light to produce the effect that would save Mlle Violetta's Parfumerie Extraordinaire.

Hastily, she added the diluent her mixture needed to attain the proper balance and consistency of perfume.

Now for the last step. Pulse ratcheting through her, Charlotte went to the shelf holding her optical lenses and filters. She pulled out the specially treated nickel oxide glass, nearly black in color. Grasping the wide plate between her hands, she carried it over to the lamp illuminating her work table.

She slid the dark glass in front of the lamp. The gaslight dimmed to dusk, strange shadows falling across her laboratory table. Her heart squeezed tight, barely daring to breathe, she turned to look at the glass bowl containing her perfume.

It blazed, like the center of a star, like all her hopes ignited, so brilliantly white she had to turn away.

Her mad gamble had worked.

She set the dark lens on the table, then sank onto her laboratory stool, her knees weak. Drawing out the golden locket she wore next to her heart, she opened it. The dear, lost faces of her parents smiled up at her—until her tears blurred everything to a wash of color and light.

THE BALLROOM at Buckingham Palace swirled with motion. At one end of the red and gold room the orchestra played for a kaleidoscope of dancers. The stark black of the men's evening coats contrasted against bell-skirted ball gowns in the palest spring hues.

A variety of clockwork animals were on display. One gentleman bore a bright blue macaw on his shoulder, while many of the women carried mechanical lapdogs. Overhead, miniature airships navigated the space beneath the chandeliers, weaving in patterns nearly as complex as the dancers below.

A cacophony of scents caught at Charlotte's nose, but she recognized her perfume and smiled a private smile. Only Queen Victoria and the inner circle of her court knew what was about to transpire.

And Sir Holcomb, who had provided assistance with the airships.

The queen presided over the celebrations from her ornate throne at the far end of the room, her husband, Prince Consort Stephan, at her side. She received a constant stream of well-wishers: dignitaries from foreign lands, other heads of state, and the highest ranks of the gentry.

As the current set of dances came to close, the queen's Master of Ceremonies rose. He beat his staff upon the parquet floor. When the room quieted sufficiently, he recited a prepared speech praising Victoria's glory and majesty.

Charlotte glanced at the liveried servants stationed beside the wall sconces. Each held a long pole with a darkened lens mounted at the very top. Most of the mechanical airships overhead had reached their positions beside the chandeliers.

The Master of Ceremonies came to the conclusion of his oration.

"Ladies and gentlemen, help me celebrate our most glorious majesty, Queen Victoria the Second!"

The orchestra struck up a fanfare, and with breathtaking precision the servants placed their filters over the bright gaslights. Overhead, the airships performed the same action, shading the chandeliers. The sudden dimness caused the crowd to murmur—then exclaim in wonder as the queen rose and progressed the length of the ballroom.

She shone as brilliantly as the full moon on a dark summer night, her satin gown glowing with silver radiance. Her ladies-in-waiting surrounded her, attendant stars underscoring the brightness of their monarch. At her side, the prince consort glimmered.

Charlotte drew in a deep breath, scented with balsam and rose and the subtle grace of the starstone. The stunned acclaim of the ballroom further affirmed that her perfume, *Jubilé d'Argent*, was an overwhelming success. Tomorrow, she had no doubt she would sell out her stock, despite the extravagantly high price.

The royals stepped onto the dance floor and the orchestra segued into a waltz. For a moment the queen and consort danced alone, but soon an entire starlit contingent of the gentry joined them. From Charlotte's vantage point, it appeared the galaxy swirled there, glittering and stately and full of promise.

Sir Holcomb appeared at her side and offered his hand. Smiling, her own gown dusted with silvery light, Charlotte accepted his invitation. Together, they stepped into the dance, another constellation turning in time beneath the violet sky.

THANK YOU, KICKSTARTER BACKERS!

This expanded edition of The Perfect Perfume was made possible by the support of the following fabulous people!

ECLECTIC COLLECTORS
Nathaniel Adams Jr

Elizabeth Anderson

Scott Chisholm

Melissa Crook

Rhel ná DecVandé

Billye Herndon

Katrina James

Jenna

John "AcesofDeath7" Mullens

Becky Naomi

Nytefyre

Jeremy Reppy

Palle Rosendahl Rømer

Shiya

Void Singer

Kerry Smith

COLLECTORS

Heather A.

Anonymous

Peter Askling

Larry "Gamerworf" Benson

Angela Blake

Amanda C.

Therena Carlin

Mark Carter

Kathryn Craig

Marie Devey

Regina Garowen

Catherine Holmes

Osmo Korhonen

Eileen M.

Sarah M

Serena M

Meyari McFarland

J.R. Murdock

Linda Niehoff

LynnMarie Panzarino

Carolyn Rowland

Vancil C Thomas

Naomi S

Seamus Sands

Leigh Saunders

Scott Schaper

Nicole Scott

John E slade jr

Jeanne Spaunburg

Myrddin Starfari

Cr5aig "Stevo" Stephenson
Rowan Stone
Melissa White
Timothy Wilson
Eron Wyngarde

SHORT FICTION FANATICS
Frank M Greco
Erik T Johnson
Katy Keller
Kari Kilgore
Pamela McNeil
Diane Muir
Michael A. Stackpole

STEAMPUNKERS
Alex
Ben P. Balestra
Kurt Beyerl,
L-rd BrayzonHead
Raphael Bressel
Penny BroJacquie
Jon Broster
Joshua A Cloniinger
Cynthia Coffman
Daryl
Hillary Griffin
Deborah Hedges
Adrienne Hiatt
Hinagirl
James Husum

Jackie

James

Jesse N. Klein

Matt & Camille Knepper

Kwynn

Larisa L LaBrant

Bo Loftis

Stephanie Lucas

Chris M

Ben Madden

Maileguy

Katy Manck

Rikard Mennenga

Adrienne Montgomery

Heidi Moone

Debbie Mumford

Caleb J. Nichols

karen flossy nightingale

Martin Oe.

Maria Owen

Dylan E Richardson

Gregory Rihn

Tyler Spencer

Star

Emma Thimbleby

Kat Tipton

Richard Valdez

ALCHEMISTS

Nicolette Andrews

Dee Astell

The Belina Family

Scott Bouchard

Derek Frank Tiberius Briggs

Cam!

Thomas K. Carpenter

Joshua C. Chadd

The Dolan Family

Juliana F

J.D.

Jess Gisler

Lotus Goldstein

Tom Gray

Jonathan Horner

Robert Jeschonek

Fred W Johnson

Stephen Kotowych

J. Jason Lau

Michelle MacQueen

John Markley

Allison Martin

Ian McFarlin

Melody

Randy Mick

Barbara O'Dell

M. Pax

Nicole Perkins

Polinchka

Erin Rakickas

Sherri Riegel

Signius

Dean Wesley Smith

Sara Crocoll Smith

Rob Vagle

Nicola W

Weston Warnock

OTHER WORKS

THE FEYLAND SERIES

What if a high-tech game was a gateway to the treacherous Realm of Faerie?

THE FIRST ADVENTURE - Book 0 (prequel)

THE DARK REALM – Book 1

THE BRIGHT COURT – Book 2

THE TWILIGHT KINGDOM – Book 3

FAERIE SWAP - Book 3.5

TRINKET (short story)

SPARK - Book 4

BREAS'S TALE - Book 4.5

ROYAL - Book 5

MARNY - Book 6

CHRONICLE WORLDS: FEYLAND

FEYLAND TALES: Volume 1

VICTORIA ETERNAL

Steampunk meets Space Opera in a British Galactic Empire that never was...

PASSAGE OUT

STAR COMPASS

STARS & STEAM

COMETS & CORSETS

THE DARKWOOD CHRONICLES

Deep in the Darkwood, a magical doorway leads to the enchanted and dangerous land of the Dark Elves~

ELFHAME

HAWTHORNE

RAINE

HEART of the FOREST (novella)

WHITE AS FROST

BLACK AS NIGHT

RED AS FLAME

SHORT STORY COLLECTIONS

TALES OF FEYLAND & FAERIE

TALES OF MUSIC & MAGIC

THE FAERIE GIRL & OTHER TALES

THE PERFECT PERFUME & OTHER TALES

COFFEE & CHANGE

MERMAID SONG

ABOUT THE AUTHOR

Growing up, Anthea Sharp spent most of her summers raiding the library shelves and reading, especially fantasy. She now makes her home in the sunny Southern California, where she writes, plays the fiddle, and tries not to game *too* much. Visit her website at antheasharp.com, friend her on Facebook, and be the first to know about new releases and reader perks by subscribing to Anthea's new release newsletter, Sharp Tales, at www.subscribepage.com/AntheaSharp